The Mystic Vial

STEPHANIE DEAN

First Edition

PAGE PUBLISHING
Conneaut Lake, PA

First originally published by Page Publishing 2024

ISBN 979-8-89315-720-8 (pbk)
ISBN 979-8-89315-738-3 (digital)

Printed in the United States of America

To my grandmother (Nanny)
A woman who, without ceasing, cheers me on, reads every chapter I write, inspires me constantly, and supports me endlessly!

Also, in loving memory of our beloved Tank.

Acknowledgments

There are so many people to thank for the creation of this book.

My incredible husband: the love of my life, my soulmate and hero. His unfailing support and unconditional love allow me to keep reaching for the stars and working toward my dreams and goals.

My grandmother (Nanny), whom this book is dedicated to. She reads every word I write and gives me constructive criticism, which makes my writing better and better.

My fabulous family. Mom and Dad (Debbie and Bill), as well as my siblings Hilary, Shane, and Amanda. They constantly cheer me on and inspire me.

My best friend Brandy. She always encourages me when the self-doubt creeps in, making me feel invincible and resilient.

My best friend Vonda, who has been my best friend since the fourth grade. We can go months without talking and then pick up right where we left off. She reminds me to take a break every now and then and giggle at our crazy antics.

Nicole Reefer and all the other folks at Page Publishing for believing in me, motivating me, and encouraging me.

Finally, *thank you*, the reader, the fan, the one that can't wait to read my next book. You're the reason I keep writing. You are the reason I keep coming up with new ideas and new stories. As long as you keep reading my books, I will keep writing them. So thank you a million times over for enjoying reading my books as much as I enjoy writing them!

Chapter One

Winston Graham sat on his back porch in a wicker chair with his laptop on his lap. It was a beautiful warm spring day. The humidity level was low and below average for South Central Alabama, making sitting outside even more pleasant. The air smelled of cherry blossoms and camellias, which had bloomed and were lining the sidewalks of the little cul-de-sac where his two-story, red-brick house was situated. The blossoms and dense trees along with the lush, green, and manicured lawns were adding bright, beautiful shades of pink, fuchsia, white, and green to the neighborhood. On the wicker-based, glass-top end table beside him was a small etched crystal glass filled with an expensive scotch on the rocks. Winston was a slim man with thinning hair. His facial features were pointed, like that of a rat, and his skin was often flushed, especially his nose, which was a side effect of his alcoholism. He reached over and swirled the beverage in his glass, watching as the ice clinked along the sides, and then took a long sip. He savored the way the scotch released the soothing heat running down his throat and filling his senses.

Winston continued to look adoringly at the image on his laptop screen. It was a stunning three-story beach house. The exterior paint was pastel yellow, and it was garnished with white shutters. The white wraparound porch that adorned the house was enormous, and Winston daydreamed of sitting on the porch daily. It was being sold for $720,000. He sighed as his husband, Fidel, walked up behind him and looked at the breathtaking house.

"If only," Fidel sighed as well, holding a stylish martini glass filled with a strong cosmopolitan.

The stem of the glass was the shape of a zigzag, and the top of the martini glass had a gleaming black rim. Fidel had silver hair, parted on the left side and combed over to the right. He was a very slender man, and he seldom walked—he glided. Almost a slither, actually. Like a snake in the grass, he would slither here and there, seeking the perfect place to curl up and wait for the thing he wanted most to strike at and devour. He wore designer glasses and designer clothes, and shopping was his passion. In fact, his shopping addiction was the only reason, truly, that he and Winston could not afford to buy the beautiful house they were ogling at.

"You know, there is nothing I want more than to buy that house and retire. Live the rest of my days sitting on that porch and watching the tide come in." Winston smiled at his daydream.

"If only we could. We can't though. We cannot afford to retire right now, Winston," Fidel said as he sat down and crossed his legs in the matching wicker seat next to his husband.

"Well, we could if my mother would help us," Winston replied.

"Do you think she would? I mean, she doesn't approve of our lifestyle, Winston. I know she tries to be accepting, and she pretends to be okay with the way we live, but she is very set in her traditional ways. Do you honestly think she would buy us a house? Especially a house at that price?" Fidel asked as he sipped his cosmopolitan, the tang causing his jaw to tingle.

"She is an old woman on the verge of senility, I think we could manipulate her into doing it. She is living with Chloe, and I think she is happy living with her. They have always been so close, but if we remind her that Chloe is a young woman and probably should be living on her own and living her own life, then Mother may be willing to move in with us."

"Wait, move in with us? Are you sure you want that?"

Fidel was not sure that Winston had thought this through. Winston constantly complained about his mother. He had said on more than one occasion that they would be putting her in a home as soon as possible. His niece, Chloe, would never allow it, however, so why on earth would he volunteer to have her live with them?

"If it gets us what we want, why not? It is not like she is going to be alive much longer. A few years at best. We could ask her to buy the house for us, and she can move in with us, and we will take care of her. We will insist it, in fact, and make sure she believes without a doubt that she will never want for anything." Winston thought he had the ideal plan.

"I'm all right with the idea if you are, I just do not know that your mother will be all right with the idea, Winston, and Chloe most certainly will not be all right with it," Fidel said thoughtfully.

"Why wouldn't they both be? This beach house is absolutely stunning. It is perfect. It's so much nicer than Chloe's little three-bedroom shack, and it gives Chloe the opportunity to live the life of a twenty-something-year-old rather than a seventy-something-year-old. She acts like an old maid, knitting and watching public television rather than partying it up, meeting new people like all other young women her age."

"Oh, Winston! I wouldn't call Chloe's house a shack. It is a cute house, for someone of Chloe's class."

"Class?" Winston asked.

"Chloe's okay, she is just not corporate like we are. In fact, we could use that to our advantage as well, I suppose. We could point out to your mother that we are better than Chloe. We are well above Chloe's class." Fidel finished his cosmopolitan.

Corporate was how Fidel classified the highest class of person. To Fidel, if you were *corporate*, you were the elite; you were the first-class, top-rate, and obviously better than everyone else.

"We would have to tread lightly on that. Mother raised Chloe after my sister died. She has had Chloe since she was an infant, and she is very protective of her. Let's hold that card in our back pocket. We won't use that unless we absolutely must. We need to play to the close relationship of Mother and her 'sainted' granddaughter. We need to remind Mother that Chloe is in her twenties and should be living a much different life than she is currently living," Winston said as he finished his scotch.

"I suppose," Fidel said.

"I'm telling you, Fidel, this will work. We will take Mother to lunch tomorrow and discuss it with her. We will tell her that we love her dearly, and since I am her son, and Chloe is just her granddaughter, that it would be in her best interest, as well as Chloe's, to live with us and let us take care of her. I will show her the pictures of the beach house and tell her that if she will purchase this house for us, then she can move out of Chloe's and move into the house with us. We will let her know that you and I will retire and take care of her. We will take her to medical appointments, we will cook for her, we will clean for her, really all she has to do is live the rest of her life as the retired famous artist that she is," Winston told Fidel.

"We will definitely want to have her envision relaxing on the porch and looking out at the ocean." Fidel smiled as he took Winston's glass to pour him another scotch.

"Oh! Definitely!" Winston smiled.

Fidel walked into the house and fixed Winston another scotch and fixed himself another cosmopolitan. When he went back to the porch, he saw Winston grinning as he relished in his own cleverness.

"Winston?" Fidel handed Winston his drink and sat next to him with his own. "What if she says no?"

"She won't."

"What if she does?" Fidel sipped his drink.

"Then we use my inheritance," Winston answered.

"That house may not be available by the time you get your inheritance."

"Of course it will be. I will get my inheritance sooner rather than later."

"How do you know? She is liable to outlive us, Winston," Fidel replied.

"I can assure you, she will not," Winston said matter-of-factly.

"What do you mean?" Fidel asked curiously.

Fidel was not sure Winston was saying what he thought he was saying; however, Winston confirmed that Fidel was correctly reading between the lines.

"You should know me well enough to know that I will stop at nothing to get everything I want," Winston answered with a sly grin. "Believe me, we will see to it that she does not outlive us."

Chapter Two

Julia Graham, an elegant and classy, wealthy widow, sat at a small square cherrywood kitchen table with a glass top, centered in a cozy dining room. In fact, everything about the house she was living in was cozy. Every room, from the living room to the three guest rooms, the master bedroom, even the bathrooms, were carefully decorated and homey. Julia was sipping a dry martini in a unique handcrafted martini glass. She had gotten the glass at a shop in Ajijic, Mexico. The stem of the glass was lime green, and the glass itself had red, yellow, blue, and purple polka dots around it. It was her favorite glass. Julia's hair was short and dark blonde, which came right out of a bottle. Her face lined with every fear, every laugh, every event she went through in eighty-four years of life, and yet she still did not look eighty-four; rather, she looked seventy-four. As she savored the taste of her martini, the smooth vodka perfectly balanced with the tang of the olive juice, she glanced at the silver watch, embedded with turquoise stones, which decorated her dainty wrist. Her granddaughter, Chloe, was working diligently in her home office, writing another book. Julia knew that soon Chloe would stop for the day and join her in the kitchen for her evening glass of wine. Would it be red or white? It simply depended on what Chloe felt like having that evening, which was why Julia would not already have it poured and waiting.

Julia Graham was a household name. She was a famous artist and her paintings sold for hundreds of thousands of dollars, and though she was technically retired, she still painted as often as possible. She was still a very vital and energetic woman after all. Painting was therapeutic for Julia, for she could put all her emotions and all her thoughts and dreams on a canvas. She took another sip of her martini as Chloe entered the kitchen.

"Hey, Nanny," Chloe said as she walked to the refrigerator and pulled out a bottle of pinot grigio.

Chloe had long jet-black hair, which today she had pulled up into a ponytail, and big, bright blue eyes. She was an attractive twenty-five-year-old, who was not yet the household name her grandmother was, but she dreamed of one day being so.

When Chloe was just a little girl, her grandmother introduced her to her first love, the written word. Chloe would devour books. She read all the time until deciding, one day, that she wanted to create her own stories. Chloe was a writer, a very good writer. She wrote books of all genres, from children's books to murder mysteries for adults, and though her books were selling, she had not had the big break she was dreaming of. Chloe was patient, though, and with the unfailing support of her grandmother, she had faith that one day her ship would come in, for with every book she wrote, her writing was getting better and better.

Chloe had a routine when she would finish the initial draft of one of her books. She would have a celebratory glass of Blue Nun 24K Sparkling Gold Champagne and sip it slowly and happily as she indulged in a steaming bubble bath. This was how Chloe would celebrate the days, hours, months, sometimes even years of revolving her life around the words she would pull from her elaborate imagination and pour them out on paper.

"I haven't seen Goliath today, honey," Julia told Chloe as Chloe sat at the table with her favorite wineglass, a blue long-stemmed glass, filled with the dry white wine. Julia was speaking of Chloe's large gray-striped purebred Highland Lynx. Chloe had gotten him when he was just a few weeks old and named him Goliath. He lived up to his name, as he was a very large cat now, but he was gentle and adored his human.

"He has been in my office with me, being lazy and sleeping in his cat bed." Chloe and Julia smiled at each other. They had an unbreakable bond. Chloe's mother, Julia's daughter, had died of an accidental opioid overdose when Chloe was a toddler, and Julia took her in and raised her granddaughter as best she could. Julia took pride in the young woman that Chloe was. After all, Julia felt it was her raising Chloe that contributed to the ambitious, compassionate, and intelligent young woman that she was.

"Ah! There he is! Come sit with me, Goliath. I have not seen you all day!" Julia exclaimed, patting her lap, as the massive gray cat sauntered into the kitchen, twitching his long tail with every step. He looked up at Julia and then looked up at Chloe as if asking permission. Chloe smiled at him, and he jumped effortlessly onto Julia's lap. He sniffed at her martini and did not find it the least bit interesting, so he lay down, pulling his tail up under his chin and between his front paws.

Julia gently pet the cat and he purred happily. "So how's the book coming?" Julia asked.

"It is coming along, I suppose. I have written four more chapters today." Chloe drank her wine slowly, as her mind was still on the book she was writing. She was working on the third book in her murder mystery series. The words she wrote would constantly fill her mind; writing was more than a passion to her—it was her obsession. She thought about whatever book she was writing at the time while she cleaned house, while she drove down the road, while she cooked delicious meals, and even while she slept, as the stories she was writing would fill her dreams.

"How many chapters are you planning on having in this book?"

"Oh, I don't know, thirty or so," Chloe answered.

"Sounds good, I am looking forward to reading them," Julia replied as the telephone rang. Julia read all the drafts that Chloe wrote and always gave her constructive criticism, which helped Chloe to become a better writer. Chloe smiled and got up to answer the phone. Her uncle, Winston, was on the other end and asked to speak with his mother.

"It is Uncle Winston," Chloe said as she handed the phone to Julia. She took the phone from Chloe and Goliath jumped off her lap. As Julia spoke to Winston on the phone, Chloe prepared supper. Goliath sat on the floor watching Chloe carefully as she cut beef sirloin into pieces for a stroganoff, hoping she would accidentally drop a piece, or two, or five or six, or even better, nine or ten! As far as Goliath was concerned, she could have a truly tragic accident and drop the entire package of sirloin. He would gladly help her clean up the mess it would certainly cause.

"Oops," Chloe purposefully said as she dropped a piece of beef on the floor and looked down at him and grinned, as he quickly ate it. He licked his chops and waited for her to drop another.

"Well, Winston, that sounds simply fine. I will meet you at the restaurant tomorrow at eleven," Julia said, then after a pause, she replied, "No, I do not need you to pick me up, I can drive. I will see you then. Goodbye, son." Julia hit the *end call* button on the cordless phone that Chloe had handed her and placed it gently down on the table next to her martini.

"Lunch with Uncle Winston tomorrow?" Chloe asked as she continued cooking supper, and every now and then she would drop tiny pieces of beef on the floor for Goliath.

"Yes, he says that he and Fidel would like to take me to lunch. What do you think he is up to?" Julia asked as Chloe took her grandmother's now empty glass to make her another martini.

"Maybe he is not up to anything. Maybe he just wants to take his mom out for a nice lunch." Chloe smiled sweetly at her grandmother.

"Maybe, but I doubt that, and so do you," Julia replied speculatively, and Chloe shrugged. "He wants something, I can feel it."

"Where are you having lunch at?" Chloe asked as she put the martini she had just made in front of Julia.

"Coleman's," Julia said as she took a sip of the martini. "That is positively delightful!" she exclaimed when she put her glass down, and Chloe chuckled.

"Uncle Winston hates Coleman's," Chloe said as she started making the sauce for the stroganoff. "You are right, he is up to something."

"Yes, but what?" Julia had no idea what her son could possibly want from her, and furthermore, she had absolutely no idea at what lengths he was willing to go to get what he wanted from her.

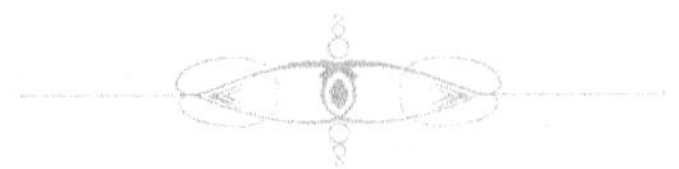

Chapter Three

Coleman's Restaurant was a classy yet cozy restaurant, with a romantic ambiance. Black iron chandeliers hung from the ceiling with flame-shaped lightbulbs, which had a fairly low wattage simulating the soft glow of candlelight. The tables were round and made of oak, decorated with rose-colored tablecloths, complementing the red-brick walls. Prints of Van Gogh, Picasso, Matisse, and even a couple Julia Graham paintings hung perfectly placed and balanced along the walls. Each table had a single white candle in the center being held by a heavy crystal candlestick, and the candles were lit every day at ten thirty by the staff, in preparation for the eleven o'clock opening time.

"She is a tough old bird, Winston," Fidel said as they waited patiently at Coleman's Restaurant. It was Julia's favorite place to eat, and Winston knew he would get brownie points for selecting it. Fidel and Winston dressed nicely for the lunch, both in khaki slacks and button-down shirts—Fidel's chocolate brown and Winston's royal blue. Both were clean shaven with not a hair out of place.

"What is your point?" Winston asked, smoothing his pants.

"Though your plan is perfect, and she most likely will choose to live with us and our fabulous corporate lifestyle, rather than Chloe's modest and humble lifestyle, she may live a lot longer than you are anticipating."

"She is over eighty, Fidel, how much longer could she be around? Besides, if we get what we want, it does not matter," Winston replied matter-of-factly, and Fidel nodded.

Julia walked up to the table and took her seat. She looked lovely in a pair of black slacks and crimson red blouse, with ruby earrings garnishing her ears. Winston and Fidel both stood to greet her, giving her a hug and a light kiss on the cheek.

"Julia, I love those earrings!" Fidel exclaimed as he sat back down.

"Thank you, Fidel." She smiled politely. She took her menu and ordered a glass of Chardonnay. Winston and Fidel already had glasses of wine in front of them. "In fact," Julia told the waitress, "I'd like to order a bottle of the house Chardonnay."

"A bottle of the house Chardonnay, coming right up, ma'am," the waitress said and left the table to fill the drink order.

"So how are things going, Mother? We have not seen each other in a week," Winston said as he looked at his menu. He really did not like this restaurant, but he was willing to find something he could, as he would put it, choke down. Yes, he would pretend to enjoy his lunch with his mother, especially if it meant getting what he wanted.

"Things are just fine, Winston. I have finished another painting, Chloe's been working on another book, and everything is just fine as frog hair. So what is the occasion?"

"Occasion?" Winston asked.

"Yes, why the nice lunch?"

"Does a son need a special occasion to treat his mother to a nice lunch at her favorite restaurant?"

"My son does," she said quietly, glancing up from her menu. Winston cleared his throat as the waitress approached the table with the bottle of Chardonnay and a glass for Julia. She took everybody's lunch order and walked away.

"Well, we did want to talk to you about something." Winston poured the wine in Julia's glass.

"Aha! I knew it," Julia said with a grin. "What is on your mind, son?"

"You, of course," Winston answered.

"Me? What about me?" Julia took a drink of her wine and savored the dry beverage as it tingled her tongue and ran smoothly down her throat.

"You are eighty-four years of age, Mother."

"You don't say!"

"Julia, please, hear Winston out," Fidel said with a sly smile at Julia's sarcasm.

"Okay, I am sorry, Winston. Go ahead, I am eighty-four years of age, and…"

"You are eighty-four years of age, and I think it would be in your best interest to move out of Chloe's house and move in with Fidel and myself. And not just your best interest, but Chloe's too. She is a young woman, after all, though she does not act like it. Don't you think that Chloe would feel more comfortable doing things that normal twenty-five-year-olds do, if she was not so concerned about taking care of you?" Winston asked.

"Winston, I am open to this conversation with you, however, I strongly suggest that you leave your niece out of it," Julia replied defensively.

"Julia, Winston and I really want you to live with us. We do not mean any disrespect and have no hard feelings with regards to Chloe. I think Winston was just trying to make a point," Fidel said.

"Right," Winston chimed in.

"All right. I appreciate that you want to take care of me, but I am really quite settled and content living where I am currently living," Julia said as she finished her glass of wine and poured herself another.

"What if you could live the rest of your days on a gorgeous wraparound porch overlooking the beautiful and majestic ocean?" Winston asked with a smile.

"Sounds lovely, sure, but I do not live near an ocean and neither do you," Julia answered, taking a sip of her wine.

"But we could." Winston pulled out a printout from his computer of the fabulous beach house he had been admiring.

"What is this?" Julia asked.

"Paradise," Fidel answered.

"I see. It is beautiful. Are you boys buying this house?" Julia asked.

"Not exactly. You see, it all depends on you," Winston answered. The table fell silent as the waitress came up with everybody's lunch and placed it gently in front of them. They all thanked her politely and waited as she walked away from the table before continuing their conversation.

"What do you mean?" Julia poured creamy ranch dressing over her large salad.

"What we mean, Julia, is that if you buy this house for us then you could move into it with us," Fidel said as he cut into his steak cooked to a medium well.

"Well, since I would be the one buying the house, I certainly hope I would be allowed to live in it."

"We would retire and take care of you twenty-four hours a day, seven days a week," Winston said as he took a bite of his club sandwich, lettuce and a slice of tomato falling out as he bit into it.

"Oh, you would, would you?"

"Of course! You are my mother and I love you," Winston answered as he dabbed his mouth with a napkin, eliminating drops of mayonnaise. "You are my mother, and it is my sole responsibility to take care of you."

"$720,000 is a lot of money, Winston."

"Can you really put a dollar amount on your well-being and happiness, Mother?"

"As a matter of fact, I can. I can tell that you have put a lot of thought into this, and for that reason, I will think about your proposal," Julia said as she ate her salad.

"That is all I ask. Just think about it." Winston took another bite of his sandwich. The remainder of the lunch was simply filled with small talk around the table as Fidel and Winston felt their plan was foolproof and would work perfectly. After all, who would choose a modest and humble lifestyle over a lifestyle of glamour and luxury? Certainly not. And if Julia did choose to stay with Chloe rather than move with Winston and Fidel, well, Winston had a back-up plan. He was going to get what he wanted one way or the other, and Fidel was all too eager to assist.

Chapter Four

Julia walked through the door of Chloe's house to see Chloe and Goliath in the kitchen. Chloe was heating herself up a bowl of leftover stroganoff for lunch.

"You haven't had lunch yet?" Julia asked looking at her watch and seeing that it was after one.

"No, I lost track of time writing until my stomach started growling. How was your lunch?" Chloe asked as she sat at the table with a bottled water and her leftovers from the night before.

"As expected." Julia smiled and sat at the table with her.

"So what did Uncle Winston want?" Chloe asked as she ate.

"Nothing you have to worry yourself about, my dear. He did make me think though," Julia answered, and he had. As Julia drove home from the restaurant, she thought about Winston's proposal indeed. She was getting on in years, and nobody lives forever. It was time. It was time for her to get her affairs in order. Were Winston and Fidel right? Had her living with Chloe held her granddaughter back in some way?

"Think about what?" Chloe asked. Goliath jumped onto Julia's lap, and Julia reacted as he expected, and she gently stroked his soft fur coat.

"Would you oppose to inviting your Uncle Winston and Fidel over for a family meeting tomorrow evening?"

"No, not at all. What about Gordo?" Chloe asked, referring to Winston's son, her cousin.

"Yes, Gordo too," she answered.

"Sure, we can have a family meeting here tomorrow night. Is everything okay?"

"Oh, everything is fine. I am getting on in years, and I think it is time to settle some things."

"Oh, no! We are not having that kind of meeting, are we? If so, then never mind, I do not want to discuss it, Nanny." Chloe got up to rinse out her bowl and put it in the dishwasher.

"What do you mean, dear?"

"Nanny, I do not want to talk about nor hear about you not being here anymore. It breaks my heart to think about it. Look at me! I am tearing up just thinking about it!"

"Oh, Chloe! Honey, it must be discussed. I am eighty-four years old. My passing is inevitable."

"Nanny, you are eighty-four, but you do not act eighty-four. You are still very active, energetic..."

"I am old, Chloe," Julia interrupted. "Just because I do not act like I am does not change the fact that I am. This is a meeting that we must have. I will call your Uncle Winston and ask that he, Fidel, and your cousin, Gordo, come over for a family meeting around five thirty, okay?"

"Well, all right. If we must. I'll whip up a nice supper." Chloe leaned over and kissed her grandmother. "I will be in my office writing."

"All right, sweetheart. I will call your uncle and then Goliath and I are going to take a nap." Julia smiled at her granddaughter as she watched her walk out of the kitchen and down the hallway into her small home office. Julia picked up the phone and dialed Winston's number. She asked that he and Fidel come to Chloe's house for a family meeting and please invite Winston's son, Julia's grandson, Gordo, to the meeting as well. Winston eagerly agreed.

Julia hung up the phone and looked down at Goliath still on her lap. "Sweet, handsome boy," Julia said to him, and Goliath yawned. "Looks like you are ready for a nap. Me too. Then I have to get things together for the family meeting tomorrow." Goliath jumped off Julia's lap as she stood up. He followed her into her bedroom and jumped onto her bed. He noticed his glorious tail and chased it a couple of times; once he caught it, he looked up at Julia expectantly, and she of course responded appropriately with a smile and scratched behind his ears. He then kneaded the bedspread and got it ready for a perfect catnap and then lay down. Julia lay down next to him and drifted off to sleep. Goliath was Chloe's cat, but Julia loved him too, and the feeling was mutual.

When Julia awoke, she decided that she would drive down to her storage unit and box up the various items she was giving her family members at the family meeting. She felt that it would eliminate any bickering, fighting, disagreeing if she went ahead and distributed things prior to her passing. She left a note for Chloe letting her know where she was so that she would not worry and then grabbed her keys and walked out the door.

Julia drove down three blocks, straight shot from the house, and pulled up to the storage unit. She unlocked the unit with her key and lifted open the large garage door. The unit was full of things that Julia had collected and acquired throughout her life, all in neatly stacked cardboard boxes and sturdy plastic totes. As she sorted through the things, old photographs, and her first few paintings, tears touched her eyes as her heart and mind were filled with memories. Memories of her late husband, the love of her life, memories of Winston when he was a sweet baby, memories of her late daughter before the drug addiction took over her life. She smiled at the pictures of Chloe when she was a little girl in her fluffy Easter dress and pictures of her grandson, Gordo, with a spoon in his mouth and covered in chocolate. She looked at her first few paintings. The paintings that jumpstarted her career as an artist. Oil paintings of beautiful landscapes—landscapes of the desert aglow by a stunning sunset, landscapes of a peaceful mountainside with a babbling creek running alongside plush trees and bushes, landscapes of a roaring ocean swallowing a white sandy beach. They each held a very special place in her heart. She went through a box of trinkets and collectibles. These things used to be in the hand-carved China cabinet that her father made for her, which now sat in Chloe's living room. They held great sentimental value to Julia as they were things that she had acquired throughout her eighty-four years. She continued to sort through everything and wiped away tears every now and then. When she finished, she went out to her car and folded the back seat down. She loaded everything into her silver sedan. She would distribute these things at the family meeting, and she would give Winston and Fidel the answer to their proposal at that time.

As Julia drove back to Chloe's house, she felt somewhat sad. She knew that when she gave her answer at the family meeting there would be disappointment, but she had to do what was best for her. She had to do what was best for her, Winston, Fidel, and Chloe, and she'd hoped with all her heart that everyone at the family meeting would understand why she had decided to do what she had decided to do.

Chapter Five

The family sat around a cherrywood glass-top dining room table. A family consisting of four people, all of whom had different motives and expectations for this family meeting.

Julia knew her time to leave this earth was near, and her estate needed to be settled and things needed to be made very clear. She knew that the three people sitting with her around this table had different ideas, feelings, and above all, expectations. She sat at the table gracefully, wearing a black dress, a heavy sterling silver necklace, and matching hoop earrings. She had rings on her fingers and her makeup was flawless, with her hair perfectly in place. As she sipped her favorite martini that sat in front of her, she watched the people around her carefully.

Winston sat quietly in his striped polo shirt and khaki shorts. His thinning hair had been freshly cut. He twirled his third bourbon in the glass in front of him. He had been waiting for this meeting all day. As the effects of the liquor took hold, he grinned at the people sitting at the table with him. It did not matter to him what his mother's wishes or intentions were. He would get what he wanted one way or the other, and he would not settle for anything less than what he wanted—not what he deserved, mind you, but what he wanted.

Fidel sat next to his husband, Winston. He would occasionally smooth out the wrinkles in his gray T-shirt and wipe his hands on his blue jeans. His gray hair modernly styled, and he had just bought his new pair of expensive designer eyeglasses. He knew his husband was about to make out like a fat rat, and he could not wait. He already had Winston's inheritance spent, though Winston was truly oblivious to it. He sipped his scotch and would smile at the thought of what was to come.

Chloe was happy to host the meeting that her grandmother had instigated. She was a great cook, and always rose to the occasion of making a delicious meal for people. She did not disappoint this evening as she had made a succulent pork loin paired with a wild mushroom risotto and fresh steamed asparagus in a white wine lemon butter. She had baked a batch of her turtle pecan brownies for dessert. After everyone had finished their meal and were enjoying their cocktails, she sat gently stroking Goliath, who was curled up in her lap, holding his tail. Chloe did not seem to mind that Goliath was leaving his hair all over her lovely green dress, as she sipped her glass of pinot grigio. She was uncomfortable with this meeting. She loved her grandmother with all her heart, and the last thing she wanted to discuss was her passing.

"Shall we begin?" Julia asked.

"Yes, let's," Winston answered, taking a drink of his bourbon.

"Well, as you all know, I am getting on in years. I do not want any confusion, disagreements, or the like when I am gone," Julia said.

"I do not see why there would be any issues," Fidel replied.

"Well, all the same, I am giving things to each of you now. Winston, I want you to have these paintings that I did. They are very important to me because they are my first paintings which began my career as a professional artist." Julia reached down and pulled up four very large paintings. They were beautiful and so intricately detailed and framed in complementing frames, which she had bought at a local craft and hobby store. She handed the paintings to Winston.

"Mother, you shouldn't have…really," Winston said in somber tone.

"Chloe, for you I have this box filled with everything that was in my China cabinet. These items hold great sentimental value to me as they are just little things that I have collected throughout my life." Julia placed the large cardboard box in front of her granddaughter. Goliath smelled the box curiously and tears touched Chloe's eyes, for the items in the box held sentimental value to her as well. She grew up admiring and adoring the small items.

"Oh, Nanny! Thank you so much!" Chloe exclaimed.

"You are very welcome, love."

"Yes, Mother. Thank you. These paintings will look beautiful in our new house," Winston said curtly.

"Yes, about that," Julia began.

"New house?" Chloe asked. "Are you all moving?"

"Julia, you haven't told Chloe?" Fidel asked.

"Told me what?"

"There is nothing to tell her. I have thought about your offer, for me to buy the beach house and move into it with you two. I appreciate the offer to take care of me, but I have decided to decline. I am perfectly happy where I am. That is all for now. Since Gordo decided not to join us this evening, I will simply put this box of things I have for him aside until I see him next. I will also be leaving my car to him at the time of my passing. My will has been updated and is in perfect order, and when the time comes, you will each be contacted by my attorney."

"Wait, that's all?" Winston asked.

"Well, yes, Winston, what did you expect?" Julia sipped her martini.

"I expected more than just a few stupid paintings," Winston answered.

"Yes, who is getting your money? Certainly, you would choose your son over…well, anyone else." Fidel glanced at Chloe as the words came pouring out of his mouth.

"It is a valid question," Winston chimed in.

Fidel continued, "After all, Winston is Julia's only child, and he has every right to know about his inheritance."

"Ah, the money." Julia smiled. "Well, that has been taken care of. It will be distributed evenly between you, Gordo, and Chloe, Winston, at the time of my death."

"What?" Fidel asked. "What do you mean?"

"Good grief, you guys, this is completely inappropriate," Chloe said, as she rolled her eyes and finished her glass of wine. She was not surprised by her Uncle Winston's reaction. She knew how selfish and greedy he and Fidel were, but she was surprised at how brazen they were. She poured herself another glass, for she felt the more wine she had, the less the people sitting around the table would frustrate her.

"Oh, shut up, Chloe. You have absolutely no right to anything of my mother's," Winston snapped.

"Well, I guess it is a good thing that I do not require nor expect anything then," Chloe retorted.

"Since the money is mine, I believe it is mine to do with whatever I want, and to give to whomever I want, wouldn't you agree? I could leave it all to Goliath if I wanted to. It is mine to do with whatever I want." Julia knew this would be an issue with Winston and Fidel. She had been watching them closely for a while and had noticed what they were doing. They were just sneaking and slithering around like a rat and a snake waiting for her to die so they could get their hands on what she spent her life saving. That is why they wanted her to buy them the beach house. Julia knew more than anyone thought she did, and she liked it that way.

"This is ridiculous! It is an absolute outrage!" Fidel jumped to his feet and threw the paintings across the room. Losing his balance, he fell to the floor. Goliath hissed at him as he jumped off Chloe's lap and trotted down her hallway to her bedroom.

"Fidel, please calm down!" Chloe exclaimed.

"Honey, are you okay?" Winston helped Fidel up. "You better fix this, Mother, you better fix this immediately!" Winston told Julia.

"Yes, indeed," Fidel replied, as he got to his feet.

"What is there to fix?" Julia asked as she nonchalantly sipped her martini.

"I think we need a timeout. It is getting late, we have all been drinking. I have fixed up a room for you and Fidel. Let's take some time, sleep, and we will discuss this in the morning."

"Are you suggesting we are drunk?" Winston asked Chloe.

"No, sir, I am not suggesting, I am saying it flat out," Chloe said as she downed her second glass of wine and stood up. Winston rolled his eyes.

"I want to finish discussing it now, right now," Winston said.

"Yes, and I think it would be best if Winston received his money now, right now," Fidel stated.

"His money?" Julia asked.

"Look, as Nanny said, it is her money and nobody else's. She will do with it what she chooses. Who cares?" Chloe asked.

"Chloe, I can't take your 'Suzy Sunshine' attitude right now. I swear, I am about to knock you into next week." Winston glared at her.

"Stop that! You will do no such thing!" Julia exclaimed.

"Look, it doesn't matter what is said, we will get what is coming to us," Fidel said calmly. "With or without your permission, Julia. There are ways around such things."

"What are you talking about, Fidel?" Julia asked.

"Well, you have to be of sound mind when a will is drafted. You clearly are not."

"All right, that is enough! I suggest we go to bed and rest until we all say something we do not mean."

"You do not have to worry about that, Chloe. I will never take back the things I say. I simply do not care what anyone thinks."

"You know, Fidel, I believe you. I, however, will most likely say something I should not. Not something I do not mean, mind you, just something I probably should not say. Now, let me show you to your room," Chloe stated calmly.

"Do not bother, we can find it ourselves!" Winston and Fidel stormed down the hallway and into one of the guest rooms in Chloe's home. Winston slammed the door, and his voice was heard through the walls, though neither Chloe nor Julia could make out what exactly was being said.

Julia finished her martini and squeezed Chloe's hand. Chloe walked with her grandmother down the hall and into Julia's bedroom.

"Good night, my dear." Julia kissed Chloe on the cheek, and Chloe held her grandmother tightly.

"Good night, Nanny. Sleep well." Chloe left her grandmother in the bedroom as she walked to her dining room and cleared the table. She picked up the paintings that Fidel had thrown across the room and carelessly left behind. She carefully leaned them up against the dining room wall then retrieved the box Julia had given her. Chloe walked down the hallway and into her bedroom where she saw Goliath lying on her bed. She put on her black satin pajamas and sat on her bed. Opening the box, Chloe looked at the beautiful trinkets, delicate keepsakes, and fragile art pieces her loving grandmother had given her. She picked up a beautiful, tiny ruby red and gold vial made of glass. She examined the vial as it was so stunning and looked antique.

"What do you think this is, Goliath? Perfume?" Chloe tried to open the vial by twisting the top. "Wow! That is on there pretty tight. I cannot seem to get it open." She twisted harder, but the vial would not open. "Oh, well, it sure is beautiful, don't you think?" Goliath yawned. "Excuse me for boring you, sir." Chloe smiled at her cat. "I am going to put this here on the dresser. It is just so beautiful." Chloe put the vial on her dresser and got into bed. She turned out her lamp, and before long, she drifted off to sleep.

Goliath, on the other hand, seemed to be wide awake. He hopped off Chloe's bed and hopped up on the dresser. As he walked the length of the dresser. his massive body bumped into the vial, and it fell to the hardwood floor shattering. Upon shattering, a blood-red haze arose from the shards of glass on the floor. It seeped out as a genie would seep out of a lamp. Intrigued, Goliath watched as the haze rose. He meowed quietly as he reached toward it with his right paw, but his paw went right through it as if he was reaching for smoke. Goliath leapt effortlessly off the dresser and onto Chloe's bed following the contents of the vial as it billowed throughout the room. He reached for the haze again, this time with his left paw, but rendered the same result. As the massive cat watched the contents of the vial fill the air, lingering and covering Chloe, he was overcome with exhaustion. He stretched, yawned, and lay down next to his favorite human. The ruby red smoke then floated up slowly toward the ceiling, still hovering over Chloe as she slept soundly. Goliath could not seem to keep his eyes open; he fell into a deep sleep while the vial's mysterious potion wafted into the air vents in Chloe's room. The blood-red haze flowed slowly through the vents filling each room in the house. Just as it did in Chloe's room, this red haze surrounded and hovered over Julia, Winston, and Fidel as they slept. For the contents of the vial would change everything.

Chapter Six

Chloe lay in bed with her eyes closed. She was contemplating as to whether she should get up. She really just wanted to roll over and go back to sleep. As she thought of doing just that, she felt a presence in her bed. She opened her eyes realizing that someone was lying in the bed next to her, Chloe leaped out of bed, as if falling victim to the electric jolt of being struck by a cattle prod. She turned to see a man asleep in the bed. She screamed horrifically, which woke the man up. He was stunned by Chloe's reaction, and he too leaped out of bed and looked around and behind him to see why Chloe had screamed.

"Who the hell are you?" Chloe asked.

The man had gray hair with black streaks, and he had stunning blue eyes. He was wearing a gray T-shirt and black flannel pajama bottoms. He continued to look around and behind him, wondering what on earth Chloe was talking about.

"Answer me! Who the hell are you and what are you doing in my bed?"

"Are you talking to me?" the man asked and then gasped. He covered his mouth with both his hands. "I am speaking human!" he exclaimed and then, wide-eyed, looked down at himself. "What happened to me?" Tears touched the man's eyes.

"What are you talking about?" Chloe asked.

"My coat! My beautiful soft gray coat!" The man was touching his body, and then looked behind him at his rear end. "And my tail! Where is my tail? My fabulous, long, glorious tail!" The man looked at Chloe, who was staring at him as if he were absolutely bonkers. "It is me, Goliath," he said. "Wow! You aged overnight. You look like an old woman."

"What?" Chloe looked down at herself and noticed she was no longer wearing black satin pajamas. She was now wearing a long-sleeved cotton nightgown with little pink roses printed on it and with lace on the cuff of each sleeve and lace on the collar. Her hands were wrinkled, and her skin seemed thin, so thin that if she bumped anything, even slightly, she would bruise. She looked behind her to find a mirror covering what should have been a wall. He was right, she was no longer a twenty-five-year-old woman; rather she was a seventy-five-year-old woman. She gasped at her reflection, mortified by what she saw. She had laugh lines around her eyes and mouth. Her long raven-black hair was now short and silver. Goliath walked up and stood beside her. He put his nose close to her and took a whiff.

"You smell the same," he said as they looked at their reflections in the mirror. "I am hideous! I was so gorgeous, and now I am hideous! What have I done to deserve such a fate?" Goliath looked at Chloe who was staring at him in disbelief. "For what it is worth, you are a very beautiful old woman."

Chloe did not say a word. She was in shock. How did this happen? What was going on? She looked around the bedroom she was in. This was not where she fell asleep. This was not her bedroom. The walls were white; her bedroom walls were lavender. She looked at the bed. It was a king-sized canopy bed. Her bed was a queen-sized brass bed. The sheets on this bed were black with a white fluffy comforter; her sheets were white with a plum-purple quilt. On the wall, where her dresser used to be, were three shelves. The top shelf held three beautiful Fabergé eggs, each delicate and fragile. One was gold with a blue sapphire stone in the middle of it, one was gold with an emerald stone in the middle of it, and one was gold with a topaz stone in the middle of it.

The second shelf held four snow globes. The first snow globe had a gold bottom with a white carousel horse wearing a Christmas wreath around its neck inside. The second was red on the bottom and inside were three hearts stacked on top of each other. The third had a green bottom and inside were leprechauns, a rainbow, and a pot of gold. The fourth snow globe was lavender on the bottom and inside were little cottontails and Easter eggs. Upon further inspection, you would find that the figurines inside the snow globes were quite alive. The white carrousel horse neighed happily as it trotted around the dome and munched on the sweet never-ending alfalfa inside, while the three hearts in the second globe would float around and often reposition themselves. The leprechauns, mischievous and ornery, would play tricks on each other, often hide the gold, and have quite an amusing time as they would slide down the rainbow. The cute cottontails in the fourth snow globe would hop around merrily and play a rousing game of hide-and-go-seek.

On the third and final shelf were two framed pictures, one on each end of the shelf. The first picture was of a small seven-year-old girl with dark brown hair and blue eyes, wearing a white peasant blouse and a long pastel pink, green, and yellow patchwork skirt. She was sitting on a stool with her hands folded in her lap. The second picture was of an older woman, Chloe, as she looked now, sitting with a man, Goliath, as he was now, and the little seven-year-old girl from the previous picture sitting between them. Where was the little girl in the photo? Where was Chloe's dresser? Where were her clothes? Where were her things? She turned and ran out of the bedroom, leaving Goliath staring at his reflection and shaking his head in utter despair. Chloe exited the bedroom to find herself in a very long hallway. The walls were covered in a burgundy and forest green striped wallpaper.

This was not Chloe's house. Panic rising inside her, Chloe ran down the hallway and through the first door she came to on the right. She entered a room and heard a soft waltz playing. In the middle of the room was a ballerina statue dressed in mint green, including the ballet slippers on her feet, in the arabesque position. The position was supported by one leg, with the other leg straight and behind the body. The ballerina's arms stretched overhead, her ceramic hands graceful and elegant. She was slowly spinning on a golden pedestal. The walls and ceiling were covered in a rich hunter-green velvet. Heavy hunter-green velvet drapes trimmed in gold thread hung on a golden curtain rod, hiding the floor-to-ceiling windows. Chloe recognized the waltz as Dmitri Shostakovich's *Waltz No. 2.* It was then that she realized she was inside a child's music box. She was filled with terror. She turned and ran out the door and back down the hallway.

She entered the next door she came to on the left. As she entered the room, she looked down, for the floor was spongy on her bare feet. She felt something stringy and slimy on her face. Disgusted, she pulled it away. She could smell pumpkin spice, a scent she immediately recognized as it was her favorite. She looked around the room to notice huge pumpkin seeds hanging from the light orange dome ceiling and walls dangling by slimy strings of pumpkin goo. Chloe was inside an enormous pumpkin. She shrieked and ran out the door. Chloe's heart was racing, and she felt as if all the oxygen and been sucked out of the atmosphere. She stood there trying to catch her breath with her back against the door.

"Wake up! Wake up!" Chloe said to herself. "I have to get out of here!" She ran down the hall to another door to her left. She went through it and immediately felt mud squish through her toes. She was in a huge garden. Larger-than-life mushrooms, carrots, and radishes surrounded her. She saw an enormous caterpillar moving around the mushrooms and disappearing behind carrot stems. She heard a buzzing sound and ducked quickly as a huge bumblebee flew over her head; it was the size of a hot air balloon. Chloe felt as if she had fallen through the looking glass. She screamed at the sight of the caterpillar and bee and ran out of the room and back down the hallway until she came to a long winding staircase going down.

She ran as fast as she could down the stairs, holding on to the rail so as not to fall, and ended up in a very large kitchen with black-and-white tiles and black cabinets with a white marble countertop. As she entered, to her right stood a large black refrigerator. Straight ahead of her was a black glass-top stove and to the left of that was a built-in double oven. To the left of the oven, Chloe saw a white door. She dashed to it, praying it was a way out. She jerked it open and saw a laundry room full of bubbles floating around and housing a front-loading washing machine and dryer. She slammed the door shut and took a few deep breaths. She could smell coffee brewing; she turned toward the counter and saw a percolating coffee pot.

"That is exactly what I need, coffee! This must be a nightmare. This stuff does not exist! Music box rooms, pumpkin rooms, twenty-foot carrots!" Chloe went to the coffee pot and quickly poured herself a cup of coffee, her hands trembling. Goliath entered the kitchen.

"I have been looking all over for you," he said.

"Goliath, I am losing it, man. I am losing my mind. I must wake up. I have to get out of this nightmare." Chloe took a long sip of coffee. Just then she saw a large rat run into the kitchen. Chloe screamed, dropping her coffee cup, which broke as it hit the tile, and she jumped up on top of the counter. "A rat! Sweet Jesus! A rat!" she shrieked.

"Help! Help! I have been bewitched! Help!" the rat was shrieking.

Goliath bent over and picked the rat up by the tail.

"Unhand me, you moron! I am a man, not a rat, I am a man, not a rat! My name is Winston! Winston Graham! Put me down this instant!"

"You do not look like Winston," Goliath said licking his lips. "You look like my breakfast." Goliath grinned and brought Winston closer to his opened mouth.

"Goliath, stop!" Chloe hopped off the counter and got a closer look.

"Oh! Thank you, sweet woman! Please, help me! I do not know what has happened. I do not know where I am or how I became this disgusting creature!"

"Uncle Winston?"

"Chloe?" Winston asked, his beady eyes blinking at her. Only one person in his entire life had called him Uncle Winston and that was his niece, Chloe.

"Yes, it is me," Chloe said staring in disbelief at the rat Goliath was holding on to.

"What happened to you?"

"I do not know," Chloe answered her uncle who was still hanging upside down.

"What year is it?" Winston asked.

"I do not know," Chloe replied.

"Put me down this instant! The blood is running to my head, I cannot concentrate on this mess! Put me down!"

"Goliath, put Uncle Winston down."

"But he looks so...yummy," Goliath answered as he eyed the fat rat he was holding.

"Goliath! You cannot eat Uncle Winston! Put him down right now!" Chloe demanded. Goliath released Winston, dropping the rat on his head.

"Ow! You idiot!" Winston rubbed his head and looked up at Goliath and then back up at Chloe. "Where are we?"

"I do not know," she answered.

"Do you know anything?" Winston asked.

"I know as much as you do. I know that I went to bed last night, and I woke up like this. We woke up like this." As Chloe said the words, a small seven-year-old girl with dark brown hair and blue eyes came running into the kitchen wearing a short-sleeved, purple cotton nightgown, with a white ruffle on the bottom, looking dazed and bewildered.

"Who are you?" Chloe asked.

"Julia, my name is Julia. Who are you? Where am I? Am I in heaven?" Julia asked and then saw Winston. She screamed in terror and ran to Chloe, leaping into her arms. "A rat! A rat! This cannot be heaven! There are no rats in heaven!"

"Julia?" Chloe asked holding on to her.

"Yes. Who are you? Where am I?" She was holding tight to Chloe's neck.

"Well, I do not know where you are, but it is me, Chloe. I am your granddaughter," Chloe answered her. She tried to put Julia down, but the little girl would not release the hold she had on Chloe's neck.

"What?"

"It is true. And the rat, that is Winston. You do not have to be afraid," she said.

"If you believe that, then clearly you do not know Winston like I do," Julia replied as she released her hold on Chloe.

"Ha, ha, very funny, Mother," Winston replied as he scurried onto the table in the kitchen. "Bring me some coffee, Chloe."

Chloe made him a cup of coffee and made herself a new cup of coffee. She poured a cup for Julia too as Julia sat down at the kitchen table. She put the cups in front of everyone and then got a broom and mop to clean up the mess she had made when she dropped her first cup of coffee. She quickly cleaned up the mess and then sat at the table.

"Goliath, you sit here by me," Chloe said to Goliath who did as he was told.

"Goliath?" Julia asked. "You are Goliath? The cat?"

"Well, I used to be," Goliath said pouting sadly.

"You are as handsome a man as you were a cat!" Julia said to him, and Goliath blushed.

Chloe sat down to her cup of coffee. She watched in disgust as Winston put his face in his coffee cup and loudly slurped the coffee.

"Well, what in the world is going on? Is this a dream?" Julia asked.

"It has to be!" Chloe exclaimed.

"Dream? It is a nightmare!" Winston replied. "Where is Fidel? What happened to him?"

"How are we supposed to know that, Winston? He is your husband. Did you not sleep next to him last night?" Julia asked.

"Of course I did!" Winston answered.

Julia, Chloe, and Winston looked at each other for a brief second and then got up from the table. Winston led them to the room that he woke up in, which was down a hallway off the kitchen. The room was different than the room that he and Fidel had fallen asleep in. When Winston and Fidel had entered the room the night before, the walls were a dark blue, and the bed was a queen-sized bed with an oak headboard and footboard. The sheets were red, and there was a blue-and-red plaid comforter. This room had gray walls, the bed was a queen-sized bed with a black wrought-iron headboard and footboard, with red sheets and a crushed red velvet blanket. Fidel was not in the bed. In fact, Fidel was nowhere to be found in the room.

"What happened to him?" Winston asked. "Where could he be?"

"He has to be around here somewhere," Chloe said. The three searched the room, but Fidel was nowhere to be found.

"Perhaps he did not get transformed. Perhaps he is not here with us at all," Julia said.

"Perhaps," Winston said sadly, and tears touched his beady eyes. "I do not know if I can handle this without him."

"Okay, okay, let's figure this out," Chloe said, and the three went back into the kitchen and sat back down at the table.

"Did you find him?" Goliath asked.

"No," answered Chloe.

"All right. We have to figure out what is going on here. How did we get in this predicament? Where are we? What year is it? How did Chloe become so old? How did I become so young? Why is Goliath such a handsome man?" Julia was just as confused as everyone else.

"And why am I a rat?" Winston asked.

"You have always been a rat," Julia answered.

"Maybe that's it," Chloe stated. Everyone looked at her quizzically. "Maybe we have become what our personalities have depicted us to be."

"What do you mean?" Goliath asked sitting at the table next to Chloe.

"I mean, Nanny has never acted like an old woman. She has always been youthful, vital, she just has never acted like an old woman. You, Goliath, always acted as if you were human. You always seemed to listen to whatever I told you. You obeyed human commands, you acted more like a person than a cat."

"And what about you?" Julia asked Chloe.

"Well, you all used to joke that I acted older than I was. You all used to joke that I was like a spinster with my sewing, knitting, and crocheting. Everyone always talked about how mature I was, maybe I have become the old woman that I act like."

"It is really cute that you thought we were joking when we told you that you acted like an old woman," Winston stated.

"Uncle Winston, you have behaved like a filthy rat and so now you are one," Chloe retorted with a tight smile.

"How dare you!" Winston was completely offended. "This is absurd. I have always been an attractive, charming man with impeccable taste and—"

"Oh, good grief!" Goliath said. "Can I eat him now?"

"No! No matter what, Goliath, you cannot eat Uncle Winston," Chloe answered him. "The real questions that need to be answered are how did we transform, why did we transform, where on earth are we, where on earth is Fidel, and how do we fix this?"

"Well, I think the first question that needs to be answered is where on earth are we?" Julia asked.

"Well, I think the first question that needs to be answered is where on earth is Fidel? If he is not here with us, then why are we here and he is not? If he is here with us, where in this house is he? What if he is lost? What if he is hurt?" Winston questioned.

"I say we start looking for him. Perhaps he has already found the answer to all of our other questions. Where are we? How did we get here? How do we get home?" Chloe stated.

Chapter Seven

Gordo Graham was the son of Winston Graham. He was invited to join his family for a family meeting at his cousin, Chloe's, house. He declined the invitation; however, he would have accepted had he known that supper was going to be served. He did not like his family, really, except for his father, of course. He loved food, though, and his cousin certainly knew her way around a kitchen. She was an excellent cook, and his mouth would water at the thought of a heavy meal and delectable dessert. Gordo would dream about food, and he ate anything and everything. Food was more than just a necessity to him—it was his obsession. This obsession was what contributed to his over four-hundred-pound physique. He awoke this morning with a craving for fried chicken and waffles, drenched in a sticky, gooey maple syrup. The thought of the crispy chicken and buttery syrup over a beautiful Belgian waffle made his mouth water.

Gordo wallowed out of bed and waddled into his kitchen. His short, light brown hair was sticking straight up. His gray sweatpants were grungy, and the black T-shirt he wore was wrinkled and barely covered his bulging belly. He heated up his waffle iron as he mixed up the boxed waffle mix. He walked to his freezer and pulled out pre-made frozen chicken and tossed it into the microwave after reading the microwave instructions on the back of the package. As he waited for his breakfast to be ready, he picked up the phone to call his father. His pudgy fingers hit the numbers on his phone's keypad. He held the phone to his ear and listened to the ringing tone on the other end. There was no answer. Gordo shrugged this off, believing that his father was probably still asleep; it was only seven o'clock in the morning after all. There was no telling how long this alleged family meeting had lasted last night.

The waffle iron beeped, indicating it was ready for him to put the waffle batter in. Gordo poured the batter into the iron, closed it up, flipped it, and waited. It beeped again, simultaneously with the microwave telling him that his breakfast was complete. He put the waffle on a plate. He wiped the small amount of spittle coming out of his mouth with his arm. He walked to the microwave and put the crispy chicken leg and chicken breast on his plate next to the waffle. He pulled a tub of butter out of his refrigerator. With a spoon clutched tightly in his hand, he shoveled a massive blob and plopped it on his waffle. He repeated the process, same amount of butter, with the chicken. Gordo then took a jug of syrup out of his cabinet. He drooled grotesquely as he poured a never-ending stream of syrup atop the waffle and chicken on his plate. He poured until pools of syrup gathered around the edges of the ceramic plate that sat steadily on his countertop. He sat at his kitchen table and dug in, smacking and grunting like a boar at the trough.

Gordo belched loudly when he finished his breakfast and grinned, sticky syrup droplets clung to his untrimmed goatee. He got up from his table and put his plate in the sink. He opened his refrigerator and guzzled down some chocolate milk right out of the carton. He picked up his phone, sat in his black recliner, and tried to call his father again. Still no answer. Gordo was starting to get concerned now. He got out of his recliner and went to his bedroom. He dressed himself in a pair of black shorts and a white T-shirt. He grabbed his keys and decided he would go to his father's house.

He got into his Chevy Suburban and drove down the road, about five miles, to his father's house. Winston's house was red brick with a white door and white shutters on the windows. There was a two-car garage with a white garage door. Gordo pulled up the driveway and noticed that his father's Cadillac was not in the driveway. Perhaps he had parked it in the garage. Gordo got out of his suburban and went up to the door. He rang the bell and waited. No answer. He knocked on the door and waited. No answer. He tried the doorknob, but the door was locked. Gordo was perturbed. He got back in his Suburban and decided to go to Chloe's house. Chloe was very adamant that when anyone was drinking alcohol, they stay at her house rather than to get on the road and drive. It was quite reasonable that his father had stayed the night at Chloe's house because drinking alcohol at the family meeting was inevitable.

He pulled into Chloe's concrete driveway that was on the left side of Chloe's navy-blue clapboard house with white trim and white decorative shutters. Gordo let out a sigh of relief when he saw his father's Cadillac in the driveway next to Chloe's blue Buick sedan. They must have stayed the night. Gordo walked up to the front door and rang the bell and waited. Again, no answer. He knocked on the door and waited. Nobody was answering. He tried the doorknob, and it was locked. He pounded on the door and waited. Gordo was now quite concerned. He walked around to the back of the house and looked through the kitchen window. The lights were off, and nobody seemed to be in the kitchen. He walked up to the backdoor and tried the doorknob. The door opened and he stepped inside.

"Chloe?" Gordo called out. "Dad? Fidel? Anyone here?" There was no answer; there was only silence. Gordo walked through the kitchen and spotted some delectable turtle pecan brownies stacked neatly under the glass dome of Chloe's cake pedestal. He grabbed a brownie, and then another, and started to stuff the brownie in his mouth as he walked down the hallway. "Hello? Anyone here?" Gordo continued to call out, with his mouth full and spitting crumbs out of his mouth as he looked into the guest rooms. The beds were unmade, so obviously his father had stayed the night, along with his father's husband. "Chloe? Where are you guys?" Gordo walked into Chloe's bedroom. She was nowhere to be found, and her bed was unmade as well.

As Gordo walked deeper into Chloe's bedroom, he noticed some glass on the floor in front of her dresser. He picked up the broken shards of glass and noticed some red residue on his fingers. Was this blood? It did not seem to be the right consistency for blood. He put his fingers up to his nose and smelled his fingers. Almost instantly, he felt dizzy and lightheaded. His stomach began cramping, and he dropped the broken glass on the floor as he put his hands to his stomach. He opened his mouth to cry out in pain; however, instead of a cry, a squeal came out of his mouth. He sounded like a pig. His eyes widened in horror as he looked at his hands turning into hooves. His nose conformed to the shape of a snout; his canine teeth were becoming tusks. He looked down and around him and noticed that he was engulfed in a red haze. He shrieked again, but it came out as yet another squeal. He was panicked as he was transforming into a large black spotted pig. He felt faint. He tried to run out of the bedroom, but he passed out before he could make it out the door.

Chapter Eight

Gordo opened his eyes, dazed and confused. He could hear Chloe's voice calling out.

"Fidel? Fidel, are you in here?" Chloe was hollering.

Gordo batted his eyes and tried to focus. He was lying on his side in what smelled and felt like wet dirt. He rolled over and walked to a pool of water. He saw his reflection and squealed at the sight of himself. He looked around and noticed he was surrounded by larger-than-life vegetables. Though they looked delicious, to his surprise, he had no appetite. He started to run, and he ran smack dab into Chloe, as she walked through the door, knocking her down on her butt! She screamed at the sight of the spotted pig that was shaking its head and doing a double take of the woman before him.

"Chloe?" Gordo was shocked to see his cousin was no longer a young lady; instead, she was a pretty elderly woman. "Chloe, is that you?"

"Yes, it is me. Gordo?" she immediately recognized Gordo's voice but was shocked to see that this was her cousin. Not only that he had transformed into a very large black-spotted pig, but that he was there in the garden room. How did he get there? He had not spent the night at her house as Winston and Fidel had.

"What happened to you?" Gordo asked. Before she could answer, Goliath, Julia, and Winston ran into the room.

"What is wrong?" Julia asked.

"We heard you scream!" Goliath exclaimed and then gasped when he saw the pig. "Stay back! Stay back, beast! Do not take another step toward my girl! I will rip you to shreds!" Goliath stood between Chloe and Gordo, hissing at him and swiping at him with his hand, as Julia helped Chloe up.

"Goliath, it is okay. It is Gordo," she said as she brushed the soil off of herself.

"Gordo?" Winston asked.

"Dad?" Gordo looked at the rat and blinked as he recognized the familiar voice of his father.

"Yes, son, it is me. How did this happen? How did you get here? How did you become a pig?"

Before Gordo could answer, Julia let out a horrific scream as a long slithering viper approached.

"Calm down, for Pete'ssssss sake! It is me, Fidel," the snake replied.

"Fidel?" Winston asked as he approached the snake. The snake slithered around Winston, quite happily.

"Yesssss," Fidel hissed, "it is me, Fidel Graham, sssssssuper sssssnake."

"Good grief," Julia said. "Winston's a rat, and Fidel is a snake, why am I not surprised by any of this?"

"I am a beautiful ssssnake." Fidel seemed quite happy with his transformation, unlike the others.

"And Gordo's a pig, I am an old woman, Nanny's a little girl, my cat's a human. I do not feel so good. I think I am going to pass out," Chloe said as she looked around the larger-than-life garden for something to sit down on.

"It is probably your blood pressure. Let's go back down to the kitchen, and I will give you some medicine. I have some in my night-stand in my room," Julia told her.

They all exited the garden room, Goliath holding Chloe's left hand, Julia holding tightly to her right hand. They got back down to the kitchen, and Julia released Chloe's hand and ran down the hall-way to the room she woke up in, as Goliath helped Chloe sit down at the table.

"Oh, no!" Julia exclaimed. She ran back into the kitchen. "My nightstand is gone! That's not all! So is my chest of drawers! My clothes, my medicine, everything, is gone!"

"Calm down, Julia. It is okay," Goliath said, rubbing Chloe's back as she was taking steady breaths in and out.

"Goliath, there's a small bathroom I saw right off the hallway, off this kitchen. Go in there and see if there's a medicine cabinet," Julia directed.

"What is a medicine cabinet?" Goliath asked. He had never heard of such a thing. A scratching post, sure. A hidey hole, of course, but a medicine cabinet?

"It is a cabinet hanging on a wall. You will know it when you see it, go look," Julia answered.

Goliath obeyed and left the group in the kitchen. He walked into a bathroom and was surprised to see the wall was covered with seashells, fish, and mermaids. He shook his head and blinked when he noticed that the fish and the mermaids were swimming on the wall. The wallpaper was alive! He started to back out of the bathroom, hissing at the wall when one of the mermaids spoke to him.

"Can I help you?" she asked. Goliath stopped and stared. "You, mister, I am talking to you. Do you need something?"

"Medicine. I need medicine for my girl, Chloe," he answered quietly.

"That cabinet there, above the sink, that cabinet has bottles of medicine in it."

Goliath walked to the cabinet the mermaid was pointing at. He opened the cabinet and looked at the bottles of medicine. It had then dawned on him that he did not know how to read. He took all the medicine bottles with him and quickly exited the bathroom and ran back into the kitchen. "The bathroom wall is covered in fish and mermaids, and they move! They move! I brought you these, I do not know what is what," Goliath exclaimed as he put the medicine bottles in front of Chloe.

"What are you talking about?" Winston asked as Chloe and Julia were looking at the medicine bottles.

"The wallpaper in the bathroom is alive!" Goliath exclaimed.

"Here, this one, Lisinopril. This is a blood pressure medication. Take it," Julia told Chloe, and she did as she was told.

"Okay, Gordo, how did you get here?" Julia asked.

"I am not sure. I was worried when Dad would not answer his phone. I went to his house, and when I realized he was not home, I got really worried. I went to your house, Chloe. I saw everyone's car there. Nobody answered the front door when I knocked, so I went around to the back. Your back door was unlocked, so I went in to check on you guys. I noticed some broken glass on the floor of your bedroom. I picked up the broken glass, and next thing I know, here I am, a filthy pig in a strange house with a fishy bathroom and a huge garden in a room." Gordo flopped down on his side on the floor when he finished, and the table shook. Everyone instinctively grabbed hold of their coffee cups still sitting on the table.

"Broken glass?" Chloe asked.

"Yeah," Gordo sighed. "It was on the floor in front of your chest of drawers."

"The vial," Chloe said as her eyes widened.

"What vial?" Julia asked.

"It was in the stuff that you gave me. It was this beautiful ruby red vial laced with gold, and I tried to unscrew the top of it thinking it was probably perfume or something, but I could not get it open. I had decided to ask you about it in the morning, so I put it on my chest of drawers, and I went to bed. How on earth did it end up shattered on the floor?"

"Um, yikes!" Goliath said.

"Goliath, what did you do?" Chloe asked looking sternly at her loyal companion.

"Well, I may or may not have, so let's not jump to any conclusions, but I probably did, knock the bottle off of the dresser last night. If I did, and again maybe I did not, but it is possible that I did, um, yeah, I might have knocked the vial off the dresser, purely by accident, but yeah, I might have done that. Yeah, okay, I probably did. Yeah, okay, I did it. This is all my fault!" Goliath hung his head in shame. "I am a bad kitty, a very bad kitty."

"Well, I suppose that is how we got in this mess. Now, how do we get out of it?" Julia asked.

"We have to figure out what was in the vial and how to reverse the effects of it. Do you know what was in it, Nanny?"

"No, but I do know what you are talking about. It had what looked like a beautiful ruby on the front of it, right?"

"Right!" Chloe exclaimed.

"No, I did not know that anything was in it. I got it at a little shop in Egypt when your grandfather and I went on vacation there. I never opened it, I just thought it was pretty and thought it would be a perfect souvenir."

"So we need to find someone who knows about Egyptian artifacts. They can tell us what was in it and how to fix this catastrophe. Way to go, Goliath, you have sent us to some crazy place and caused us to transform into disgusting creatures. I always thought you were a stupid cat! I never understood why Chloe loved you so much and—" Winston was interrupted by Chloe.

"That is enough! It was an accident, that is all, an accident that needs to be resolved."

"I am not stupid," Goliath said sadly.

"No, Goliath, you are not stupid. Nanny and I will get dressed and explore this world that we are in. Goliath, you will come with us. Uncle Winston, you, Gordo, and Fidel will stay here," Chloe said standing up.

"Why can't we go?" Fidel asked.

"Because I do not want to draw attention to us," Chloe answered.

"Yes, it would be quite bizarre to be seen walking around town with a pig, a rat, and a snake. But how are we to get dressed to go out in public? We have no clothes here," Julia answered.

"Well, all we know is that we do not have our clothes here. There may be clothes in the closets. We will have to look," Chloe answered.

Chloe, Julia, and Goliath walked back to the rooms where they woke up. Chloe opened the large closet door in her room and saw several cardigans hanging neatly, all a different pastel color. Next to the hanging cardigans was a chest of drawers. The first drawer she opened contained T-shirts of the same color as each cardigan. The second drawer contained long broomstick skirts all matching the T-shirts and cardigans. On the floor of the closet were two pairs of sandals, one pair white and one pair black, as well as a pair of black men's shoes and a pair of brown men's shoes. Next to the chest of drawers were men's cardigans, all in a dark color. Then next to the cardigans was another chest of drawers. Chloe opened the drawers to find men's pants, dark in color and folded neatly. Chloe opened another drawer and found matching T-shirts. Chloe pulled out a plum-colored cardigan, plum pants, and a black T-shirt and laid them neatly on the bed, while Goliath watched her curiously.

"There, Goliath. A perfect, distinguished outfit for you."

Chloe chose a lavender cardigan, a lavender skirt, and a white T-shirt. She dressed herself and slipped into the white sandals. Goliath picked up the cardigan that his human laid out for him and smelled it. He tossed it on the bed as he picked up the pants and smelled them too. He looked at Chloe and then looked back at the clothes.

"What is wrong with you? Get dressed, we have to go," Chloe told him.

"How?" Goliath asked.

"What do you mean?"

"How am I supposed to put these things on?"

Chloe realized that Goliath had never worn clothes before, nor did he ever dress himself. Chloe picked up each garment and explained to Goliath how to put it on.

While Chloe was in her room, explaining to Goliath the art of dressing himself, Julia opened the closet in her room and saw the same things that were in Chloe's closet, with the exception of size and men's clothes, though she did not know it. Julia chose a lavender cardigan, skirt, and white T-shirt. She, too, slipped into the white sandals that were in her closet and was surprised to see that everything fit her perfectly.

"Ah, to be young again. How marvelous," Julia said with a smile as she admired herself in the mirror.

She turned and exited her room to find Chloe and Goliath walking toward her.

"Well, don't we look absolutely precious in matching outfits," Julia said with a smile when she saw Chloe was wearing the same outfit as she was. "And you, Goliath, how handsome you look in your plum outfit," she continued.

"You think so? Chloe picked it out for me, and then told me how to put it all on. I was not sure about it, but if you think it looks good then, I suppose it does." Goliath smiled.

With that, Julia, Chloe, and Goliath got themselves ready to explore this new world that the contents of the mystic vial had put them in.

Chapter Nine

Julia, Chloe, and Goliath said goodbye to Winston, Fidel, and Gordo as they stepped outside. It was a warm day, yet cloudy and gray. The air was dry, so unlike the humidity the three were used to being from South Central Alabama.

"My word! I can tell I am going to need lotion here. It is dry, very dry, like a desert. Do you think we are in the desert? Maybe a southwestern state, like New Mexico or Arizona? Maybe we are in western Texas. The enormous vegetables in the indoor garden, you know, everything is bigger in Texas," Julia thought out loud, and Chloe shrugged. She had no idea where they were, but she too noticed the difference in climate.

They walked down the steps at the front of the house and through a six-foot heavy silver gate. As the three stepped out, they looked around. They stood on a black-and-white brick sidewalk, laid in a fishbone pattern. The houses surrounding them were painted either black or white. As they continued on the sidewalk, they turned and looked at the house they were living in and were surprised to see it was neither black nor white, for it was gray. An enormous gray stone house, with gray pillars and a large wraparound porch. There were huge windows on the top story going all around and two large windows on the lower level at the front of the massive home.

"Well, I will be damned," Julia said. Goliath and Chloe both looked down at her. "In a world of black and white, there is indeed a shade of gray," she said.

"Nanny, while we are out and about, we should probably keep in mind that you do not look like a mature woman anymore," Chloe said, as they slowly walked down the sidewalk.

"Right, you look like a little girl," Goliath chimed in.

"And?" Julia asked.

"And it is inappropriate for a child to say things like 'I will be damned,'" Chloe responded.

"Oh, yes, I suppose you are right. I will have to be more careful," Julia said.

The three turned right at the end of the block to find themselves in a bizarre town. Bizarre indeed. A colorful town, it was not, for all the storefronts and business buildings were also painted either black or white. The black-and-white brick sidewalk was never ending on each side of a brown cobblestone street. Trees lined the sidewalk, with gray trunks and tan leaves, and the treetops were covered in bubbles. Thousands of bubbles were floating through the air.

"There is a bug stuck in that bubble!" Chloe exclaimed as a bubble floated toward her. "I think it is a dragonfly." Chloe reached out to the bubble, and it popped.

A pixie dressed in silver emerged from the bubble and buzzed up to Chloe's nose, causing Chloe to go cross-eyed.

"Do I look like a dragonfly to you? I am a pixie, you twit!" the pixie said angrily.

"I am sorry, I did not mean..." Chloe was stunned and apologetic.

"You should not jump to conclusions. We pixies do not appreciate being confused with insects!" The pixie stuck her tongue out at Chloe and flew away.

"Snippy little thing, isn't she?" Julia looked up at Chloe and continued looking around at the bustling street. "How cute! Look at that fellow over there." Julia nodded her head in the direction of a bald man dressed in a chocolate brown cardigan walking a ferret on a leash. "His pet is wearing a matching outfit! How adorable!" In fact, a lot of people were walking pets on leashes, and all pets were wearing cardigans that matched that of their owners.

"Look! That fellow has a frog on his shoulder, and he is wearing clothes!" Goliath pointed at someone else.

As they walked, a woman walking a small dog on a leash, both wearing pink cardigans, passed closely to Goliath, and Goliath hissed at the small dog, causing the woman to jump, but the dog seemed undisturbed.

"Goliath, stop. You cannot hiss at things. You do not look like a cat anymore, remember?" Chloe told him.

"Of course I remember, how could I forget? But how am I supposed to make other creatures believe that I am dangerous if I cannot hiss at them? How do I keep them away?" Goliath asked.

"Well, humans usually don't care about seeming dangerous, but if they want someone to stay away from them, they usually say something like, 'Please don't invade my space,'" Chloe answered.

"Frankly, telling Gordo you would rip him to shreds certainly got your point across," Julia said.

The street was very busy with people walking about. All of whom were wearing cardigans of different colors, with the men in pants and the women in broomstick skirts. Chloe, Goliath, and Julia walked down the sidewalk doing their best to avoid bumping into people as they walked.

"Do you smell something?" Goliath asked as he sniffed the air.

"I do, and I am glad you do too. I thought I was having a stroke," Julia replied.

"It smells like cookies," Chloe said.

The air was filled with the aroma of cinnamon and sugar. The scent of freshly baked cookies surrounded them.

"It is making me hungry. We should have brought Winston with us. I could have snacked on a part of him. You said I could not eat him, you said nothing about snacking. I could eat an arm or a leg," Goliath said quietly.

"Goliath, no! Leave the rat alone." Chloe smiled as she said it.

"Um, Chloe?" Goliath asked.

"Yes?"

"People are staring at us as they walk by," Goliath answered.

"Of course they are. We look fabulous," Julia replied as she smiled and nodded at the people.

"I do not think that is it," Chloe responded as she noticed that the people were really looking at them, more shocked than admiringly. She was so busy looking at the people walking around her, she did not notice the woman walking in front of her, and they bumped into each other. "Oh! I am so sorry! Excuse me!" Chloe said to the lady.

She was a thin woman with short blonde hair and brown eyes. She was wearing a red cardigan and broomstick skirt with a black T-shirt and black sandals. Her makeup was flawless, and Chloe could not help but notice her perfectly lined eyes, volumized lashes, and her lipstick was the identical shade of red as her outfit.

"Oh, think nothing of it. I simply was not paying attention and…" The blonde woman stopped as she looked at Chloe. "Oh, my word!" she exclaimed.

"What is wrong? Are you hurt? Did I hurt you?" Chloe asked.

"No, not at all, it is just…you must be new here in Snickerdoodle."

"Snickerdoodle!" Julia exclaimed. "Isn't that just charming!" Everyone looked down at Julia for a brief second, and she smiled sweetly at them all.

"Snickerdoodle?" Goliath asked.

"Yes, Snickerdoodle. I am Petunia Picklepick. And you ladies are in violation of our dress code and could get a ticket."

"A ticket? For what?" Chloe asked looking around. "Cardigan, T-shirt, skirt—we are all dressed the same."

"Oh, dear! Come in here with me." Petunia showed them into a small shoe store. The group of four stood in the doorway as Petunia explained. "Today is September tenth. Monday was September seventh. Labor Day."

"And?" Goliath asked.

"And you, sir, are dressed appropriately, but you ladies are wearing white sandals."

"That is illegal? Wearing white shoes after Labor Day?" Chloe could not believe that anyone still abided by such an old-fashioned faux pax.

"Wearing anything white from the waist down. It is strictly enforced here."

"Why?" Julia asked.

Petunia blinked, clearly surprised by the question. "I do not know, it just has always been that way. It is also the law that everyone wears a cardigan, which all three of you have done. So we must get you two a pair of black sandals," Petunia told them.

"I have black sandals, I just thought white went better with what I am wearing," Chloe responded.

"I do too, but I think we should just get another pair while we are here, rather than risking getting a ticket going back to the house," Julia responded.

"With what? We do not have any money," Chloe whispered to Julia.

"No money?" Petunia was surprised. "Who are you people?"

"Well, I am Chloe Graham, and this here is Julia and Goliath."

"Chloe Graham? The Chloe Graham?" Petunia asked wide-eyed.

"Um, yes, Chloe," Chloe answered suspiciously.

"Well, then you, ma'am, have plenty of money. In fact, you are the wealthiest person in Snickerdoodle. I know because I am the president of Snickerdoodle National Bank. I have taken it upon myself to oversee your account so that you get the special attention that you so deserve. As you know, you have been making several large deposits for years. It is so nice to finally meet you face to face." Petunia smiled at Chloe.

"Yes, well, thank you. I am so thrilled that I made the right decision in banking with you," she told her, knowing she must play along.

"We just moved into our house here," Julia said.

"Ah, yes, the only gray house in Snickerdoodle. I should have known it was you. Anyone with your money can afford to beat to a different drum." Petunia chuckled, and Chloe smiled at her.

"I am so confused," Goliath whispered to Julia, and Julia shrugged.

At that moment, a short balding man wearing a black cardigan over a red T-shirt and wearing black slacks approached the group.

"Good morning, Petunia," he said.

"Good morning, Mr. Cobblebrook," Petunia replied. "This here is the Graham family. Ms. Chloe and…" Petunia looked down at Julia.

"Julia, Julia Graham. I am her granddaughter."

"Of course. Ms. Chloe and Miss Julia need a pair of black sandals, and I am afraid Ms. Chloe has simply forgotten her purse. Would you mind opening a line of credit for them?"

"Certainly, certainly," Mr. Cobblebrook said. He then led the ladies to an aisle full of black sandals. "Let's see, Ms. Graham, I believe you are a size seven, and little Julia, I think you are a size four." He pulled boxes of sandals off the shelves as Chloe and Julia sat down on the white padded benches. Goliath watched curiously.

"Well, all, I will leave you in Mr. Cobblebrook's most capable hands. I must get to work. Please come see me when you are done here. The bank is three blocks down on the left." With that, Petunia sauntered out the door.

Once Chloe and Julia had their new shoes, they stepped out of the shoe store to the busy sidewalk. They heard the sound of large flapping wings and were shocked when they instinctively looked up.

"Is that…," Chloe started.

"Well, I will be! That is a unicorn!" Julia exclaimed as the three watched a massive white winged unicorn fly overhead. It was one of four, flying together. One was black, one was spotted black and white like a paint, and the third blonde like a palomino, all with golden horns and golden hooves.

"Where on earth are we?" Chloe asked unable to take her eyes off the beautiful unicorns.

"Perhaps we are not on earth, Chloe," Julia answered.

Chapter Ten

While Chloe, Julia, and Goliath were exploring outside, Winston, Fidel, and Gordo were exploring the massive house they were in.

"Should we split up?" Fidel asked.

"Absolutely not!" Winston exclaimed. "We should stay together. We could get lost. We could get sucked into some black hole for all we know."

"I agree," Gordo stated.

They began exploring, starting in the bathroom. As they went into the bathroom, they saw that Goliath was right. The wallpaper was alive! Clown fish, sting rays, blue tang fish, and sea turtles were swimming happily. Even the anemones and seaweed were swaying as if being moved by invisible currents of salty ocean water.

"Ah, there you are." The mermaid that had spoken to Goliath was now speaking to the three animals who all jumped when they saw her. She had flowing, long black locks of hair, green seashells covering her breasts, and a blue-black fin. Glowing, golden eyes were looking out at Winston, Fidel, and Gordo, who stood before her, their mouths all opened in awe.

"You are a mermaid…in a wall," Winston said to her as he got a closer look.

"Well, technically I am on the wall, but, yes, right now I am a mermaid."

"What do you mean right now?" Gordo asked.

Suddenly, the mermaid let out a loud and wicked laugh! Gordo squealed; Fidel slithered behind Winston who had screamed like a prepubescent girl. Lightning flashed and thunder roared as thick black smoke engulfed everyone and everything in the bathroom. When the smoke cleared, the three terrified creatures were no longer in the bathroom, for they found themselves in the oversized garden room hovering close to each other next to a broccoli plant the size of a small hedge!

"How did we get back in this garden?" Fidel asked.

"I d-d-do not know, but I am f-f-frightened!" Winston stammered.

As they looked around them, a huge ladybug scurried up. "Boo!" she said to them and cackled again. They all screamed and ran in separate directions. Winston scurried behind a carrot, Fidel slithered and coiled up behind a radish, and Gordo ran as fast as he could, taking cover behind a toadstool.

"You cannot hide from me, fools!" the ladybug said, as again lightning flashed and thunder roared, and again the thick black smoke emerged. They miraculously ended up in the music box room.

"This is lunacy! Lunacy, I tell you!" Winston exclaimed, quivering beside the ballerina statue, spinning slowly on the pedestal. "What in the world is going on here?"

The ballerina stopped turning, and she came to life. She put her leg down and hopped off the pedestal. She walked slowly up to Winston, who was backing away and up against the velvet wall, where Gordo had found himself, and Fidel was quickly approaching. She did a fouetté, grand jetted, and plied across the floor to the animals.

"I am Lonora," she said. "I can be what I want to be when I want to be. I am a mermaid swimming along in the bathroom, I am a ladybug or bumblebee or even a snail in the garden, I am a beautiful ballerina here in this music box room, and I can be a pumpkin seed in the pumpkin room. I can put myself in paintings, I can creep around like a spider or fly." Lonora spun and transformed into a tall woman with long black hair and dark eyes, wearing a black dress, low cut in the front revealing her cleavage, and slits on the side of the skirt going up to her thighs. A slender Elvira-esque woman. She slowly walked away from Winston, Fidel, and Gordo and sat, cross-legged, on the pedestal and ran her black polished fingernails through her hair.

"You are a witch!" Gordo exclaimed.

"Some have called me that, yes."

"Lonora. What a fabulous name. Lonora," Fidel said as he slithered toward her.

"Fidel! Get away from her, she is dangerous!" Winston whispered loudly. Fidel ignored him as he slithered up and around Lonora's arms. Lonora smiled.

"Indeed, I am. But not for you three. I am your ally," she said as she delicately ran her fingers down the viper's long body.

"Ally?" Winston asked as he stepped closer, seeing that he was in no immediate danger.

"Yes. I know more than you think I do, and I can spy on everyone here. That woman and little girl are far too goody-goody for my taste, and that large man…well…what a scaredy-cat! However, you three. I can see that you three are more my type. I am powerful, very powerful, and I choose to use my powers to get what I want, when I want." Lonora leaned down and was eye to eye with Winston, a black polished nail under his chin ever so lightly. "You can use my powers to get what you want, if you want."

"Type?" Gordo asked.

Lonora removed her finger from Winston's chin as she answered, "Greedy, selfish, dark hearts. Yes, you are definitely my kind of creatures." Lonora laughed again, evilly, and transformed back into the ballerina turning in circles on the pedestal. Fidel slithered over to Winston and Gordo who were watching her, no longer afraid but intrigued.

"Don't you see? She can spy on Chloe and Julia for us. She can find out where Julia's money is. She can help us. Do you seriously not see how she can help us?" Fidel slithered around them.

"Well, Lonora, I think this may be the beginning of a truly beautiful friendship." Winston grinned slyly.

Chapter Eleven

Julia and Chloe were in their new black sandals carrying their white sandals in a bag, staring in awe at the flying unicorns overhead.

"I sure hope one of those things does not get the urge to poop! Bird poop is bad enough, but could you imagine unicorn poop?" Julia asked.

"Do you think unicorn poop is sparkly?" Goliath asked, considering Julia's observation.

"Well, I suppose we better go to the bank." Chloe chuckled at Julia and Goliath then changed the subject. "If I am the wealthiest person in this town, I must have thousands in there," Chloe said.

"Oh! Chloe, dear." Julia laughed. "Thousands? You must have millions."

"Millions?" Goliath asked. "What does that mean?"

"Thousands of dollars is not what a wealthy person has. Upper class, maybe, or as Fidel would say, 'corporate.' Wealthy people, the really wealthy people, have millions," Julia answered.

"You really think so?" Chloe asked as she dodged the bustling people on the street.

"I know from experience, dear."

As the three walked down the street, they could see the bank. It was a large white brick building with black pillars in the front and black molding over the front entrance. In the molding, engraved in white letters, SNICKERDOODLE NATIONAL BANK. They walked through the doors and stepped into a large lobby with a white marble floor, a couch, and four wingback chairs all upholstered in a heavy, black-and-white striped fabric. To their left were several small offices, and to their right, a row of small booths where tellers were working diligently.

"May I help you?" a red-headed, green-eyed teller asked them.

"It is fine, Anastasia, they are here to see me," Petunia replied as she walked toward them from her office. "Please, follow me into my office." The three walked toward Petunia's office. "You look much more appropriate now in your new sandals," Petunia said as they entered the office. Petunia's office had a large cherry-oak desk, three white wingback chairs, and a large black filing cabinet. The trio sat in the chairs. Chloe sat between Julia and Goliath. "Here you are, Ms. Graham." Petunia handed Chloe a thick file.

"What is this?" Chloe asked as she opened the file.

"As soon as I got in to work, I made a copy of your entire file for you." Petunia smiled.

"Thank you," Chloe said, then nearly jumped out of her skin when she saw the large orange bearded dragon sitting on Petunia's desk. The dragon was wearing a red cardigan and seemed content in his location.

"Is that a…," Chloe started.

"That is Alfonso. He is my baby. He won't harm you, he is a very sweet bearded dragon," Petunia replied, as Goliath, wide-eyed, held back a hiss.

"How very nice of you to copy that file for her," said Julia.

"Well, I would do anything for my favorite customers," Petunia smiled.

"Favorite?" Goliath asked.

As Chloe examined the contents of the file, she saw the deed to their house, bank statements, a will, letters from a realtor, and letters from an attorney. Julia looked on and grinned.

"I am also assuming you will need to make a withdrawal so that you have some cash on hand. I have already ordered you a new debit card and you should have that in a few days."

"Thank you so much," Chloe said as she continued to look through the file.

"Of course, of course. So how much would you like to withdraw?"

"Um…" Chloe looked at the most recent bank statement, and her eyes widened and nearly popped out of her head. She looked at Julia who was seeing the same thing she was and smiled. Four hundred twenty-five million dollars!

"Umm, I guess two thousand would do for now," Chloe said quietly.

"Sure, I am sure you have cash stashed away in your safe at home too." Petunia smiled as she got up from her desk.

"Um, yes, of course I do," Chloe replied.

"I will be right back." Petunia left her office.

As soon as she was gone, Chloe pointed to the balance and looked shockingly at Julia.

"That is right. That is how much money is in the account," Julia smiled.

"Nanny! What is all this?" Chloe asked.

"Well, it seems to me like the money that I had in our world has been moved over here to this world, and since you are now the matriarch, and I am the child, you have the money now."

"Wait, you have nearly half a billion dollars?" Chloe asked.

"Well, I did, now you have it." Julia smiled and patted Chloe's hand. Goliath started to sniff. He sniffed the air, then his hands, then his arm, then under his arm.

"What is wrong with you?" Chloe asked.

"I smell something. I think it is me," he answered.

"You smell fine to me," Chloe told him.

"No, no, I absolutely do not. I need a bath." Goliath licked the back of his hand and rubbed the back of his hand over his face. He licked the back of his hand again and was about to run it through his hair when Petunia walked back in the office. Chloe grabbed Goliath's hand and put it down on his lap. Goliath looked at Chloe with a pout.

"Here you are." Petunia handed an envelope with cash to Chloe, completely oblivious to Goliath's odd behavior. "What else can I do for you today, Ms. Graham?"

"I think that will be it for today, Ms. Picklepick," Chloe answered as the three stood from their seats. Chloe extended her hand, and Petunia took it in return as Chloe stated, "Thank you so much, Ms. Picklepick."

"Of course, and please, call me Petunia. I like to think of my customers more like family and friends. If you need anything else, please do not hesitate to let me know." Petunia smiled as she said it while the three prepared to exit the office. Chloe nodded, and she, Julia, and Goliath exited the bank.

"So what do we do now?" Chloe asked Julia when they walked out the door.

"Well, first, I suggest we go talk to that Jefferson Addlebock. He is your lawyer," Julia said, indicating the name seen on Chloe's will and letterhead in documents that were in the file. The three of them walked down the street looking for Addlebock, Attorney at Law.

While Chloe, Julia, and Goliath were learning about this new reality, Gordo, Fidel, and Winston were hatching a devilish plan with Lonora.

"So, Lonora," Winston began, "where are we?" Winston sat in the music box room, cross-legged, stroking his whiskers.

"You are in the town of Snickerdoodle, living in the largest, most expensive, and only gray house in this town." Lonora spun slowly on the pedestal, in the arabesque position, as she spoke.

"Snickerdoodle? That sounds delicious," Gordo responded.

"The town is known for the popular cookie," Lonora replied. "There is a bakery on every corner, and each bakery claims to make the best, but the truly best snickerdoodle cookie is made by the Crocker Bakery. It is owned by Elfkin Crocker."

"Who caressss?" hissed Fidel.

"I care!" Gordo exclaimed. "Perhaps we could get Chloe, Nanny, or Goliath to pick us up some cookies. I could go for some cookies. The stress of this situation has me seeking comfort. Comfort in a soft, warm cookie covered in cinnamon and sugar." Gordo drooled a little as he spoke and then grunted and snorted.

"Gordo, we are not interested in cookies, we are interested in my inheritance, and that is it. All we care about is the money that I am entitled to," Winston told him.

"Ah, yes, the money," Lonora said with a grin. "First of all, you need to understand that the money does not belong to this person called Nanny. It belongs to the old one."

"The old one?" Fidel asked.

"You mean Chloe?" asked Winston.

"Yes," Lonora answered.

"Oh my gosh!" Winston laughed loudly and evilly. "Do you realize what this means?" Winston looked at Fidel and Gordo. "This will be like taking candy from a baby!"

"Yay! Candy!" Gordo exclaimed.

"Gordo, focus!" Winston continued. "Sweet, naïve, people-pleasing Chloe! She would do anything to make us happy! She desperately wants to be loved and accepted. She won't think twice about giving us the money. She is probably the easiest person on the face of the earth to manipulate!"

"Yessss!" Fidel slithered around happily. "But do you think she knows about the money? Do you think she knows that she has it? Chloe is not the brightest bulb, if you know what I mean."

"I am sure she'll figure it out while she, Nanny, and Goliath are out there searching this world we are in," Gordo answered.

"Lonora, do you know where the money is?" Fidel asked.

"I am sure the majority of it is in the bank, Snickerdoodle National, but there are several hiding places here in the house. I am sure that I can find out where and what the ignorant old woman is hiding. I can follow her around without her even knowing. As long as she is in the house, that is." Lonora winked at Winston.

"Brilliant!" Winston exclaimed.

"Wait! What about when she is not in the house? Why can't you follow her when she is out of the house?" Fidel asked.

"I have no power outside this house. It is a very long story why, I won't bore you with the details, but the point is I cannot leave. However, how hard would it be for a rat or snake to follow her outside of these walls?"

"Excellent," Winston whispered.

While this disgusting plan was being hatched and discussed, Julia, Chloe, and Goliath met with Mr. Jefferson Addlebock.

"I must say, Ms. Graham, it is such a pleasure to meet you in person," Jefferson said. He sat behind a black marble desk and swiveled in a white leather chair. He was a slender man with light brown hair and green eyes with a light brown goatee on his face. A large painting of the attorney hung on the wall behind him.

"Yes, you as well, Mr. Addlebock," Chloe replied quietly as Julia and Goliath sat in the lobby patiently waiting for her. "We have recently moved into our house here, and I am just meeting with everyone, making sure that all my affairs are in perfect order. I would like for you to just clarify some things for me."

"Of course, of course." Jefferson opened a desk drawer at the bottom of his desk and pulled out a large file. He opened it up and began going over everything that was in it. "Let's begin with your will. Any updates?"

"Oh, yes, my will. Well, let's see here." Chloe opened the file that Petunia had given her and found the copy of her last will and testament. "It says here that the bulk of my estate will be divided equally between Julia and Winston."

"Correct. That is to include everything in the bank, as well as the diamonds and everything else you have in your safe at your house," Jefferson said.

"Where do you see that? I do not see that here," Chloe said as she reviewed the documents.

"Well, it is not really broken down there. You had indicated, when we drafted this will, that you would let Julia and Winston know about everything and where everything is."

"Yes, of course I did. I'm so sorry, you must forgive my forgetfulness." Chloe smiled at the attorney.

"Not a problem at all, that's what I'm here for," he responded with a warm smile. He was a kind man, not at all what Chloe had expected. She worried that he may be a money-hungry, scheming creep. He was, thankfully, the exact opposite. "We could certainly redraft the will to be more specific. Would you like me to do that?" Jefferson continued.

"Please do. In fact, I would like you to redraft this will to indicate that everything goes to Julia at the time of my death. I will not be leaving anything to Winston. It is all hers, after all," Chloe stated.

"All hers?" Jefferson asked.

"Um, yes, well, it will be. That is what I meant. It will all be hers," she rephrased remembering that Julia was at the present time a seven-year-old little girl.

"Okay. Well, let's discuss everything that is in your estate, then shall we? You have the house." Jefferson took out a legal notepad and started writing everything down.

"Yes, about the house. I see the deed here, but I don't see the accompanying paperwork. Do you have that?" Chloe asked.

"Yes, ma'am. I have it here. In fact—" Jefferson stopped short and pushed a button on his phone.

"Yes, Mr. Addlebock?" a friendly female voice spoke on the speaker.

"Rita, please be so kind as to make a complete copy of the Ms. Graham's file for her. I have it here," Jefferson answered her.

"I'll be right in, sir." Rita was in the office in a flash and took the file from the attorney.

"So back to the will. You would like to leave the house to Julia." Jefferson Addlebock went right back to business.

"Yes, the house and everything in it," Chloe said.

"Including the safe and the contents therein," Jefferson said as he wrote.

"Yes, the safe. Everything in my accounts at Snickerdoodle National."

"And the safety deposit box?" Jefferson looked up at her.

"The what?" Chloe started sifting through the papers in her file.

"The safety deposit box. I believe you stashed away several assets in there such as your jewels, some emergency cash, and I think that is where you put some of your most important documents. Your passport, social security card, birth certificate, etcetera."

"Um, no, sir. I no longer have that safe deposit box. I see here on this document that I closed that quite some time ago." Chloe showed Jefferson a document with her signature on it.

"Ah, yes. You must have moved those things into your safe."

"Yes, of course I did. The closer the better, don't you agree?" Chloe was getting the hang of playing this act.

"Absolutely. Well, then, your diamonds, rubies, sapphires, and emeralds will all be left to Julia."

"Exactly. All of my assets will be left to Julia. How long will it take you to get this revised will drafted?" Chloe asked as Rita walked back into the office with the copy of the file for Chloe. "That was fast!" Chloe was surprised at the efficiency. Rita smiled sweetly at her and walked out of the office and back to her desk.

"I should have it drafted and ready for you to sign by tomorrow morning." Jefferson smiled.

"Wonderful, just wonderful! I will come by, say, around nine tomorrow morning?"

"Perfect," Jefferson said as he and Chloe stood in unison. Jefferson walked Chloe out of his office and smiled at Julia and Goliath as they stood up. The three walked out of the attorney's office and down the street.

"Well?" Julia asked.

"Well, a new will is being drafted leaving you everything. Where would I put a safe?" Chloe asked Julia.

"A safe?" Julia asked.

"Yes. Apparently, I have a safe filled with jewels, cash, and important documents."

"Well, of course you do! It used to be in a safe deposit box, but I moved it into the safe that is hidden in my closet. Well, what used to be my closet, in another world," Julia replied.

"Then it must be in a closet in the house here, somewhere in that house," Goliath replied.

"We better get back to the house and find it before Winston and Fidel do," Chloe said as they crossed the street and hurried back home.

Once they arrived back at the house, Chloe called out when they walked through the door, "Uncle Winston? Fidel? Gordo? We're back." Chloe waited for a response, but there was none. "Uncle Winston?" Chloe hollered again. She looked down at Julia and shrugged.

"Well, I will go search in my room, you and Goliath search in your room, and we will take it from there. I am sure Winston and

Fidel are around here somewhere, so watch your back," Julia said in a whisper. Julia walked into her room and looked around. She looked under the bed and behind all the doors, making sure there was no rat or snake sneaking around. She then opened her closet and began searching for a small safe.

As Chloe and Goliath walked into Chloe's room, Goliath let out a loud and long hiss as he stared at a painting of a beautiful woman with long black hair and emerald green eyes hanging above Chloe's bed. The portrait showed that she was wearing a black top with a high collar made of lace. Every hair on Goliath's head, every hair on his arms, every hair he had stuck straight up.

"What is wrong with you? It is a painting. A beautiful painting at that," Chloe said to him as she looked closer at it.

"Beautiful?" he asked. "I do not think it is beautiful. I think it is creepy. There's something about it. I do not like it. Was it there this morning?" Goliath asked and he hissed at it again.

"Stop that! I am sure it was. Paintings do not just appear and disappear, Goliath," Chloe said as she looked under the bed and behind the dressers. "Uncle Winston? Fidel? Are you guys in here?" she asked as she searched. They were nowhere to be seen in the room. Chloe opened her closet and pushed the clothes aside. She felt as if she was being watched. She turned around and scanned the room with her eyes. Goliath was still staring at the painting. Chloe started knocking quietly on the back wall of the closet. Suddenly, she heard a different sound. She looked behind her again to make sure that she was not being spied upon. Goliath noticed.

"What is wrong with you?" he asked as he stepped up beside her, turning away from the painting.

"I am just being paranoid, I guess," Chloe pushed on the wall and a twelve-by-twelve part of the wall flipped around, exposing a twelve-by-twelve fireproof metal box. "Holy crap!" Chloe exclaimed. She looked around again.

"Is that it? Is that the safe?" Goliath whispered. Chloe got down on her hands and knees and looked under the bed again. She got up and walked to the window and looked behind the curtains. "What are you doing?" Goliath asked.

"I feel like I am being watched," Chloe said. She shrugged and walked back over to the closet. She gently put her hand on the top of the box as she looked for a way to open it. However, when she put her hand on the top of the box, it opened. "That's awesome!" Chloe exclaimed in a whisper. Chloe and Goliath both looked around them. Chloe looked closer into the box and gasped as she saw the precious gemstones, a pile of cash, a passport, and a manila envelope marked IMPORTANT DOCS in black marker.

Chloe was right, of course. She was being watched. She was being watched very closely; she just did not realize it. For as Chloe and Goliath had their back to the painting that Chloe thought was so beautiful, the woman in the painting blinked and an evil smile touched her lips.

Chapter Twelve

The rubies, diamonds, sapphires, and emeralds gleamed in an array of colors that mesmerized Goliath. He reached his hand in the safe, and Chloe slapped it.

"What do you think you are doing? Do not touch!" Chloe scolded him.

"But they are so pretty! I want to play with them. I think these things could keep me well occupied for hours on end," Goliath said staring at the jewels, his pupils aglow with the different array of colors.

"No! Do not touch them." Chloe pulled out the envelope that was marked IMPORTANT DOCS. She opened it and examined the contents. A copy of the will, the deed to the house, some bank statements, a copy of the check that paid for the house, her birth certificate, a birth certificate with Julia's name on it, a birth certificate with Goliath's name on it, her passport, a passport for Julia and a passport for Goliath, and certificates of authentication with regards to the jewels. She put them back in the envelope and put the envelope back in the safe. Goliath never took his eyes off the jewels. Chloe looked confused as she examined the safe.

"What is wrong?" Goliath asked.

"How do you close this safe?" Chloe asked. She put her hands on the sides of the safe and the top closed up. "Wow! That is awesome!" Chloe smiled at Goliath.

Goliath put his hand on top of the safe. Nothing happened. He looked at Chloe, puzzled. Chloe put her hand on the top of the safe and it opened. She put her hands on the sides, and it closed up. "How fun!" she exclaimed. She gave the safe a light push, and it flipped back into the wall. She put the clothes back in order and closed the closet door. "Let's go find Nanny and tell her what we found."

Chloe started to walk out the door with Goliath behind her. Goliath turned to the painting and hissed again as they walked out the door.

While Chloe and Goliath were discovering the safe, Julia was going through her closet looking for the safe, but she found much more. Julia moved clothes around and knocked on the wall. She found nothing of interest. She got down on her hands and knees and looked around on the floor. She found something in the corner. It was a silver laptop.

"Well, look at this," she stated as she picked it up. When she picked up the laptop, something else caught her attention. There seemed to be a hidden trapdoor under the laptop. Julia looked around and behind her to make sure nobody was spying. She lifted the trapdoor and found a straight staircase leading down. "This must lead to a basement," she whispered to herself. Julia slid the laptop under her bed and then went down the staircase, closing the trapdoor behind her. As Julia crept down the dark staircase, she placed her hand on the wall, not only to steady herself but she was hoping to find a light switch. Her hand was gently rubbing the wall with each step she took when something hit her on the face. She reached up and realized it was a thick string. Julia gave it a tug and a lightbulb shone brightly, illuminating the staircase. When Julia reached the bottom of the stairs, she gasped. She had found herself in an elaborate artist's studio. The walls were painted in bright and vibrant colors of hot pink, lime green, and a rich purple. They were lined with shelves containing both oil and acrylic paints of every color, as assortment of canvases, and brushes of every style and size. There was a very large easel and a smaller easel next to it. Julia explored the studio with glee. She felt like a kid in a candy store. She saw pencils, markers, sketchpads, and transfer paper. She could not help but smile from ear to ear. She was inspired, truly inspired, and she could not wait to create a masterpiece in this perfect studio. She raced back upstairs to tell Chloe what she had found. She raced through the trapdoor just as Chloe and Goliath were walking into her bedroom and closing the door behind them.

"We found it!" Chloe exclaimed.

"Fabulous! Come look what I found!" Julia bounced up and down joyfully as she pointed to the trapdoor. Chloe and Goliath followed where she was pointing with their eyes. "It leads to the most amazing studio you could possibly imagine. Everything any artist would need to create masterpiece after masterpiece!"

"Cool," Chloe said.

"Oh, and that is not all! Look at this!" Julia reached under her bed and pulled out the laptop.

"Fantastic!" Chloe exclaimed. "We can use the laptop to research the vial! Please take it to the kitchen. I am going to find Fidel, Uncle Winston, and Gordo. We need to have a family meeting so we can tell them what all we found out today."

"Are you going to tell them everything?" Julia asked.

"Well, not everything." Chloe winked, and they parted ways.

Chloe called for Winston, Fidel, and Gordo as she searched the rooms in the house. She finally found them in the garden room. Winston was munching on a huge lettuce leaf, Fidel was slithering around, and Gordo was rooting through the soil.

"Chloe! You're back!" Winston announced. Gordo looked up and then went back to the soil.

"Yes, sir, we are going to have a family meeting downstairs in the kitchen, come on. We have a few things to tell you guys." Chloe turned and walked out toward the stairs and down to the kitchen with Winston, Fidel, and Gordo hurrying behind her. They were very anxious to hear what she had to say, hoping that they were going to hear that she was giving them millions. Winston scurried up on the table, Fidel slithered up next to him, and Gordo sat on the floor.

"We are in a very interesting place, boys," Julia began.

"Yes, a town called Snickerdoodle," Goliath said.

"Yeah, yeah, named after the cookie which they are famous for. What else?" Fidel asked impatiently. Winston eyed him and Fidel then realized he was not supposed to know that, for that was information given to them by Lonora. "I mean, snickerdoodle is the name of a cookie, so I would assume that is why the town is called that." He tried to cover.

"Anyway," Julia continued, "they have a very strict dress code here."

"Yes, and everything is in black and white, it's not a very colorful place. The buildings, the furniture, everything. Everything, that is, except for our house, which is gray," Chloe said.

"Yawn! Boring! What else?" Fidel was so very impatient.

"Nanny found this laptop, and we are going to use it to research Egyptian artifacts and see if we can find out about the vial, or at least maybe someone who can help us," Chloe said.

"Yes, and I also found a studio to paint in, so I am going to create a painting, duplicating the vial so that we have a visual aid," Julia replied.

"And?" Winston asked.

"And there are unicorns! Unicorns flying around! People walk around with pets dressed just like them. This place is bizarre!" Chloe replied.

"Do not forget about the snippy pixies!" Goliath exclaimed.

"Oh, yeah! There are pixies here, they move around in bubbles, and the bubbles cover the trees and float around everywhere! That is about it, that is about everything we found out," Chloe informed them.

"What do you mean?" Winston asked.

"Well, there are some shops and businesses and a lot of people," Goliath stated. Then Goliath yawned a huge yawn and stretched. "I am sleepy. I am going to go find a place to take a nap," Goliath said getting up from the table. He left the kitchen and went up the stairs.

"So, yeah, that is really all we can share for now," Chloe said.

"Ugh, well, that is nothing!" Winston said with a pout. "Nothing! Absolutely nothing!"

"Unicorns and pixies, Uncle Winston! Do you seriously not think that is something? Unicorns and pixies!" Chloe told him and he shrugged. "While we were gone, did you guys learn anything more about the house?" Chloe asked.

"The house?" Winston asked. "Well, Goliath was right about the bathroom. Other than that, nothing really that you did not already know about," Winston lied.

As the meeting continued downstairs, Goliath looked for the perfect place to take a nap. He walked into the music box room. He stepped in and sighed contently at the soft music playing. He walked up to the window and stepped behind the heavy green velvet drapes and gazed out the window. Goliath yawned and had decided that this would be the perfect place for a nap, but as he was about to step out from behind the drapes, he heard the door open, so he stayed put.

"Chloe knows nothing of the money!" Winston shrieked as he walked into the room.

"Lonora? Lonora?" Fidel called out. As he did, the familiar black cloud of smoke filled the room, and Lonora appeared. Goliath stayed hidden, though he could hear and see everything. His eyes widened as Lonora stood before Winston, Fidel, and Gordo. He held back a hiss but could not keep the hair on himself from standing on end.

"Lonora, we are going to need your help. Chloe is not bright, I am afraid, and she knows nothing about the money," Winston told Lonora.

"I told you she is not the brightest bulb, Winston, she's just plain dumb," Fidel said.

"Of course, she knows. She knows everything," Lonora said. "Speaking of Chloe, I would certainly hate for her to walk in and see me." Lonora spun in a cloud of smoke and transferred herself into the spinning ballerina in the middle of the room. Goliath's eyes widened even more, and it was even harder to hold back his typical reaction to something so dark and evil.

"What do you mean?" Gordo asked.

"Oh, darling, I am afraid that Chloe is brighter than you think. She knows that she has money. She also has found a safe in her closet."

"What is in the ssssafe?" Fidel asked.

"I could not see exactly. I know she saw an envelope, and there seemed to be something bright and colorful. Maybe jewels, I could not see inside the safe. The idiot man and the old woman were in the way. I could not see inside without giving myself away."

"That little sneak!" Winston exclaimed. "I bet she is planning on keeping everything to herself! I am shocked! That is so unlike her."

"Ssssso, Lonora, you are immortal, right?" Fidel asked.

"Only one can destroy me, but she is not a problem anymore," Lonora said, and Goliath listened intently.

"Who is not a problem?" Gordo asked.

"Amethyst," Lonora answered, spinning slowly on the pedestal in the middle of the room.

"Amethyst? Who is Amethyst?" Gordo asked.

"Amethyst is the witch in the backyard. I trapped her in a tree." Lonora laughed wickedly. She stopped laughing and grew silent suddenly as the door opened and Chloe poked her head in.

"Have you guys seen Goliath? He said he was going to take a nap, but I cannot find him anywhere."

"He is probably in your room," Winston answered Chloe.

"No, he is not. I looked in there. I think he is scared of the painting in there."

"He is ssssuch a sssscaredy-cat!" Fidel hissed. Goliath's jaw dropped. He was shocked that Fidel would say such a thing.

"Well, can you guys help me look for him? I would really hate for him to get lost in this house," Chloe said, and with that, the three followed Chloe out of the music box room to search for Goliath. Nobody knew that Goliath was hiding in the music box room, listening and seeing everything that was going on.

Chapter Thirteen

The spinning ballerina shook violently as Lonora emerged. She stood in the music box room in her sleek black dress and long black hair to her waist. She looked around her. She felt as if eyes were upon her. She sniffed the air and could smell something was off but could not put her finger on it. She lifted her hands, palms inward, and was engulfed in black smoke, and like that, she was gone.

Goliath came out from behind the drapes, muttering to himself as he walked across the room slowly toward the door, "Scaredy-cat! You are the scaredy-cat, Fidel! Scaredy-cat! I will show you scaredy-cat! You won't be calling me a scaredy-cat when I am ripping you to shreds!" Goliath stopped and took a deep breath. "Although now I am a human, I do not really have my claws. I will karate chop you, Fidel!" Goliath said as he did a karate chop in the air. "Yeah, karate chop! Scaredy-cat this, you jerk!"

Goliath made his way outside, still muttering to himself and imagining how he was going to obliterate Fidel. He continued to karate chop the air, and every now and then, he would throw in a kick, until he made his way around the house and into the backyard. In the middle of the yard was a tall willow tree. Goliath stopped his fantasy and stared at the tree. He walked up to it and looked closer. He could swear he could see an eye in the trunk. He put his nose close to the trunk and smelled the tree. He then put his hands on it and spoke to it, "Hello?" There was no response. Confused, Goliath scratched his head.

While Goliath was outside examining the willow tree, Chloe was inside searching for him.

"So, Chloe, are you sure there is nothing else you want to tell us? There's nothing else you discovered in town that you want to share?" Winston prodded.

"Yes, I am sure. Goliath? Where are you, silly beast?" Chloe was starting to worry about her most loyal companion.

"Positive?" Fidel asked.

"Yes, I am positive," Chloe answered as she looked out the window at the end of the hallway. "There he is, he is outside in the back of the house! What is he doing outside?"

"Because, you know, Chloe, you could tell us anything. We would never betray you," Winston said.

"Sure, I know that. I am your only niece, we are family, why on earth would you betray your only niece? I mean, I love you so much, Uncle Winston. Of course, I know you would not betray me. You do not betray your family," Chloe said with a smile, knowing full well that Winston, Fidel, and Gordo would throw her off a cliff if it benefited them. "Thanks for helping me look for Goliath." Chloe trotted down the stairs and walked through the kitchen. She walked into the laundry room and found a backdoor. She stepped outside and saw Goliath staring at the willow tree.

"Amethyst? Are you in there?" Goliath asked the tree in a hushed whisper.

"Who is Amethyst?" Chloe asked Goliath and he jumped.

"Oh, hi. Uh, nothing. Nobody." Goliath wanted to find out what was going on before filling Chloe in on what he heard in the music box room.

"What are you doing out here? I have been looking everywhere for you," Chloe said.

"Nothing. Just checking out this willow tree. It is nice, isn't it?"

"Of course. I love willows. They are beautiful trees."

"Yeah." Goliath continued to stare at the tree.

"Well, look, I am going to go in and use that laptop Nanny found to research the vial. Do you want to come in?" Chloe asked.

"No, it is a nice day. I think I will stay out here for a little bit," Goliath answered.

"Okay, well, be careful and stay close to the house. I do not want you getting lost."

"Okay, I will," Goliath said as Chloe turned to go back into the house. "Chloe?"

"Yeah?"

"You be careful too. Do not trust anyone. Well, except for Julia, of course," Goliath said, and Chloe smiled and nodded at him as she walked back into the house.

Once Chloe was back in the house, she opened the laptop and turned it on. The screen flashed and up on the screen came a box that said *pin*.

"Oh, bummer. I need a pin number," she muttered to herself and put her head in her hands as she thought of what the pin number could possibly be. "Okay, my birthday is November 21." Chloe typed 1121. A screen popped up INCORRECT PIN. "Of course, that is too easy. Um, Nanny's birthday is December 28." Chloe typed in 1228. INCORRECT PIN. "Crap! I only have one more try before it locks me out for good," Chloe said to herself, and she thought very carefully.

She looked around the house for any numbers that may catch her attention but found nothing. She looked out the window and could see Goliath still inspecting the willow tree. She typed in 0602. The computer flashed up the home screen. "Yes! Of course, I would use Goliath's birthday!" Chloe looked down at the bottom righthand corner of the screen and saw the little icon indicating that the laptop was connected to the internet. She moved the little arrow on the screen down to the Google Chrome icon on the bottom of the screen and tapped the laptop. The Google homepage appeared on the screen. She went to the search bar and typed in EGYPTIAN ARTIFACTS and hit Enter. She scrolled through the results that came up on the screen but did not see what she was looking for. She went back to the search bar and typed EGYPTIAN ARTIFACTS WITH RED STONE and hit Enter. Though she learned what red means to the Egyptian culture, she still found nothing with regards to the vial. She sighed and looked up at the ceiling. "Okay," she started typing as she spoke, "where can I find Egyptian artifacts and historical information in Snickerdoodle?" She hit Enter and the screen came up referring Chloe to the Snickerdoodle University. Chloe moved the little arrow on the screen and tapped the computer when it was on the Snickerdoodle University website, and there she saw that Snickerdoodle University had an Egyptian history and cultural studies class. Chloe got up from the table and looked around for a pen or pencil and some paper, going through drawers and cabinets. As she was searching, Julia came into the kitchen holding a painting she had created of the vial.

"What do you think?" Julia asked Chloe as she showed her what she had painted.

"Hey! It is perfect!" Chloe smiled. "It looks exactly like the vial!"

"It does, doesn't it? And it has inspired me to paint again." Julia admired her work. "What are you doing?" Julia asked Chloe.

"I am looking for a piece of paper and a pen or pencil so that I can write down the name and address of someone who might be able to help," Chloe answered as she opened drawers and investigated cabinets.

"There's paper and pens and pencils in the studio. I will go get some. Here, take this. Be careful, it is still a little wet." Julia handed the painting to Chloe and ran down to the studio.

"Amazing for a seven-year-old!" Chloe exclaimed to herself as she smiled at the painting.

Julia returned to Chloe with a sheet of paper and a pencil. Chloe took it from her and laid the painting gently on the counter. She went back to the computer and jotted down the information she had received: LIAM DONNELSON, PHD; SNICKERDOODLE UNIVERSITY; CONWAY HALL; ROOM 403; SOUTH AVENUE K; SNICKERDOODLE, ODDITY.

Chloe folded the piece of paper and handed the pencil back to Julia.

"Okay, I am going to see if I can meet with this Dr. Liam Donnelson at the university here. Do you want to go with me?" Chloe asked Julia as she closed the laptop.

"No, I think I am going to stay here and do some painting," Julia answered.

"Whatever you want to do, have fun. Goliath is in the backyard having a conversation with a tree," Chloe said as she got up from the table.

"A tree?" Julia asked.

"Please do not ask me to explain the behavior of a cat turned human, I have given up understanding anything at this point." Chloe leaned down and gave Julia a kiss before walking out the door. Julia shrugged and went back downstairs to the studio.

As Chloe left and Julia went down to the studio to paint, Goliath yawned. It had dawned on him that he never did get that nap he needed. He thought maybe if he took a nap on one of the branches on the willow tree, something would come to him. Goliath carefully climbed up the willow tree and situated himself belly down on a thick branch. He rested his head on his hand and drifted off to sleep.

While Goliath was napping, Julia entered the studio and looked around. She noticed a door to what looked like a closet. She opened the closet door. Julia gasped and covered her head as a few paintings fell out and onto the floor.

"What is this?" she asked herself and lifted one of the paintings. "Wow! This is a brilliant piece of abstract work!" she exclaimed as she examined the abstract painting with awe. "I know this is not anything I have done, I am not an abstract artist." She looked for the mark of the artist and her jaw dropped when she found it. "I'll be damned!" she exclaimed as she saw, etched in the painting: Chloe Graham.

While Julia was discovering the hidden talents of her granddaughter, Winston, Fidel, and Gordo were discussing how to manipulate her.

"I told you this would be easy," Winston said as he sat cross-legged in the pumpkin room.

"I do not understand, I always thought you had a good relationship with your niece," Fidel said as he coiled up next to Gordo who was munching on an enormous pumpkin seed.

"Please, Fidel! I do not care enough about Chloe to have any relationship with her. I just know that she would do anything for her family, and she will do anything to make me happy. Believe me, she loves me far more than I have ever loved her. She is probably just waiting for the right time to tell us about the money. You know, when Mother is not around," Winston replied.

"So what is the plan?" Gordo asked.

"We are going to utilize our relationship with Lonora," Winston began. "We are going to find out exactly how much there is and then we will manipulate Chloe into giving it all to us. She will feel like it is her responsibility to make sure that we are taken care of and that we receive what is rightfully ours. She is so eager to please she will be easy to manipulate."

"You never cease to amaze me, Winston." Fidel grinned slyly.

"I never cease to amaze myself with my cunning wit." Winston returned the grin.

As the plan against Chloe was being discussed, she walked into the lobby of Conway Hall at Snickerdoodle University. The outside of the hall was white brick and the pillars in front were black-and-white striped. As Chloe entered the lobby, she saw a sign indicating the professors who worked in the building and their office numbers. She walked down a hallway looking for office number 403. She came to a closed black door with the number 403 painted in white on it as well as LIAM DONNELSON, PHD. Chloe knocked on the door.

"Come in," a man's voice was heard. Chloe turned the knob and entered the office. Sitting behind a large black desk was an attractive man. A very attractive man, a silver fox, with gray hair and hazel eyes. Chloe took notice of how attractive the man was, and she felt a blush come over her.

"Hi. I am looking for Dr. Donnelson," Chloe said quietly.

"I am Liam Donnelson," the man replied. He could not help but notice how beautiful the woman who stood before him was. Her bright blue eyes and perfect skin. He wanted to know the story behind the laugh lines that were around her eyes. Chloe noticed a painting that hung behind him and stared at it for a minute, for there was something very familiar about it.

"My name is Chloe." Chloe extended her hand for a handshake, and Liam returned the gesture.

"Chloe, I am Liam. Of course, you know that. You came to my office looking for me." Liam laughed nervously.

"Yes," Chloe smiled, "I need to talk to you about something that you may find completely bizarre, and I am truly hoping that you do not think I am insane."

"I am intrigued," Liam responded. "Have a seat here." Liam pulled out a chair upholstered in black corduroy. Chloe took the seat and watched as Liam sat behind his desk.

"Do you know what this is?" Chloe handed Liam the painting that Julia painted.

"It is a very nice painting," Liam answered.

"Yes, it is, but do you know anything about the vial that the painting depicts?"

"No, should I?"

"So here's what happened. My grandmother gave me this vial, and my cat knocked it off my dresser in the middle of the night. When he did that, something happened. Something came out of that vial and transported my family and myself here. And that is not all. Not only did we get transported here, but we also became different people…things…different."

"What?" Liam cocked his eyebrow.

"I am not a seventy-five-year-old woman. I am a twenty-five-year-old woman. My grandmother was transformed into a seven-year-old girl, when in reality she's an eighty-five-year-old woman. My cat was transformed into a human man, my uncle a disgusting rat, his husband a snake, my cousin a pig. Those three transformations are not too far from reality, but the point is, I do not understand it. This is not who we are, and this is not our world, and I want to go home. I want to go back to my world with my cat and my grandmother, and if absolutely necessary, my uncle, his husband, and my cousin." To Chloe's surprise, tears touched her eyes as she spoke.

"So what makes you think this vial would be something I would know about?" Liam asked Chloe and handed her a tissue.

"My grandmother got the vial in Egypt while on vacation. I thought that since you were a professor of Egyptian history and culture, you might know what it is. You might be able to tell us how to reverse the effects of this vial." Chloe dabbed her eyes with the tissue.

Liam felt sorry for her, though he was not sure whether her story was true or if she was, in fact, crazy.

"I will tell you what, let me look into this vial and I will see what I can find, okay?" Liam smiled warmly at her.

"Okay, that sounds great." Chloe sighed a sigh of relief, just at the thought of someone trying to assist her, and she smiled back at him. "I will check back in with you in a couple of days if that is okay." Chloe stood up.

"Sounds wonderful." Liam stood and opened the door for Chloe.

"Thank you so much, Doctor."

"Please call me Liam," he said as Chloe walked out the door. She smiled at him as she walked away, and he closed the door behind her.

Chloe got back home and walked through the front door of the house feeling tired and emotionally drained. Julia ran up to her.

"Chloe! You must come see what I found!" Julia grabbed Chloe's hand and led her down to the studio. "Look! Look what I found!"

"What are these?" Chloe asked, picking up and looking at the paintings.

"They are brilliant abstract paintings!" Julia exclaimed.

"Yeah, they are nice," Chloe said.

"Honey! Look at who the artist is!" Julia pointed to the artist's mark, and Chloe looked on wide-eyed when she saw Chloe Graham.

"I painted these?" Chloe was astonished.

"You are a famous artist, my dear!"

"But I am not. I can't be."

"Why not?" Julia asked. "Here, do not answer that. You just sit here next to me and paint. I am working on a painting of Goliath, as he used to be. You paint whatever is in your heart. Paint whatever you want." Julia put a canvas on an easel in front of Chloe. She gave her some paints and brushes and a palette. Chloe began painting.

While Chloe was inside painting, Goliath yawned, stretched, and rolled over, forgetting that he was up in the tree and down he went to the ground, breaking a small branch on his way down. Goliath sat up and shook his head while dusting himself off. He looked at the tree and saw what looked to be a drop of something flowing freely from the "eye" of the tree trunk. Goliath stood up and placed his finger to the droplet. It was a tear. It was not sap, or dew, but an actual teardrop.

"Oh, no! Did I hurt you, Amethyst?" Goliath asked the tree. "Amethyst, can you hear me? I do not know how to get you out of that tree!" Goliath sat down hard on the ground and some soil around the base of the tree moved. Goliath looked closer and underneath the soil was a ruby red stone. Goliath put his hand on the stone, and the ground beneath him began to shake as if an earthquake or volcano had erupted. He immediately removed his hand, and the ground stopped shaking instantly. Goliath looked around to see if anyone had witnessed what he had. He put his hand back on the stone, and the ground shook again. This time Goliath did not move his hand.

The wind began to blow furiously, and the leaves on the willow tree and all other trees around flew along the current of the strong wind. As the ground shook violently, the tree trunk started to miraculously break open, as if it were a hatching egg. A bright golden light filled the area where Goliath was, illuminating all that was around him, wind still blowing and howling, the ground still trembling and shaking. There was a rumble in the atmosphere as if there were a strong thunderstorm in the distance.

Goliath's eyes widened as the bark on the tree began to fall all around him. The wind never died down, the earth never stopped quaking, and the light seemed to shine brighter and brighter, until finally, a beautiful woman with long, flowing auburn hair and sparkling lavender eyes emerged. She was dressed in a lavender gown, and her ebony cheeks shimmered as if covered by silver glitter. The wind abruptly stopped blowing, as if it had never been blowing in the first place. The light vanished, as if it had never been shining. Everything was quiet and still, except for the beautiful woman who had emerged. Goliath blinked his eyes in astonishment at her as she turned to the broken tree and placed her hands on the stump, which was all that was left of the trunk. A bright lavender glow came from her hands and the beautiful willow tree was miraculously put back together and looked as if nothing at all had happened to it. She bent down and picked up the ruby red stone that Goliath had touched. Lavender light glowed from her hand once again and engulfed the stone. Goliath could not believe his eyes, for the ruby red stone turned to dust and fell through her fingers and to the ground beneath their feet.

"Thank you, kind sir, for releasing me. I will be forever in your debt!" the woman said to Goliath. Her voice was soft and melodic.

"Are you—" Goliath began but the woman interrupted.

"I am who you are seeking, but we must not talk here. Follow me, and I will tell you everything you need to know," the woman said as she walked away from the tree and down a narrow path. Goliath followed her, turning every now and then to make sure they were not being followed by a rat, a snake, or a pig.

Chapter Fourteen

Amethyst walked down a narrow pathway slowly and gently, with her palms facing the ground. As she walked, a light lavender hue glowed from her hands. With each step she took, beautiful flowers immediately grew along the pathway. Flowers of all types—daisies, petunias, marigolds, even tulips—had burst and bloomed through the earth. Amethyst and Goliath walked under a white metal arch and entered a gorgeous flower garden. The air smelled of a mixture of roses and carnations. Honeysuckle vines crawled along the garden. There were benches, fountains, and statues, all made of concrete, and the statues were in the shapes of cherubs, butterflies, birds, and gnomes.

"Wow! This is beautiful!" Goliath exclaimed as he walked into the garden. He was in awe. He joyously started hopping and skipping through the garden. He just could not contain himself. The lovely flower garden made him feel very happy.

"Thank you." Amethyst laughed at Goliath as she watched him frolic through the landscape. Once he stopped, she gestured for him to sit on a bench.

"Did you do all this?" Goliath asked as he sat down.

"I did. I did this a very, very long time ago. There was a time when Snickerdoodle was vibrant and full of color," Amethyst said quietly. Her voice was sweet and soothing. She looked around and admired the garden but then sadness touched her face as she remembered what used to be. "I created this garden, and I created the house that you are living in."

"Who are you?" Goliath asked.

"I am Amethyst. I used to be a very, very powerful fairy."

"Used to be? Seems to me like you still are. Fairy? Aren't you a little big to be a fairy?"

"Not at all." Amethyst smiled gently. "Fairytales and stories make fairies out to be small pixie-like characters. That is what makes them stories, you see, it is not true. Fairies are simply just people who have special talents, special magical powers."

"Oh. I am kind of new to this human stuff. Do all humans know that? Are fairies everywhere?" Goliath was enjoying this time with Amethyst. He liked her. He felt happy and warm being in this place with her. "I mean, maybe Chloe is a fairy. She has a lot of special talents, and if she ever scratched you behind your ears or rubbed your belly, you would swear she had magical powers."

Amethyst laughed. "No, silly. Chloe is not a fairy. She does, however, have a beautiful heart. As does Julia and as do you. The three of you have a very kind spirit."

"You know all of us?"

"I know who you all are. You are new to being a human, because in another world and at another time, you were a cat."

"I was! I was a gorgeous cat. I was probably the most gorgeous cat in the whole world, but I made a huge mistake and broke something in Chloe's bedroom and now I am this. I have lost my beautiful fur, my fabulous tail, all of my handsomeness is gone, gone, gone!" Goliath pouted.

"You are still handsome, friend. And though you may not look the same, you still think the same as you did before. You are still just as clever and just as brave and just as amusing as you were before." Amethyst smiled and gently put her hand under Goliath's chin. "But you, Julia, and Chloe, are in grave danger. The others have evil hearts. Dark hearts, filled with greed, selfishness, envy, and malicious motives. You all must be very careful, and now that I am free, I can help you all."

"You think I am brave? Fidel called me a scaredy-cat."

"You are very brave, my friend." Amethyst chuckled.

"Are you speaking of the other lady? The one that spoke to Winston, Fidel, and Gordo?"

"I am speaking of Lonora, yes, but I am also speaking of that Winston, that Fidel and that Gordo."

"Well, I believe that about…what did you call her…Lonora? I also believe that of Winston and Fidel, but Gordo? All he thinks about is food. That is all Gordo cares about."

"Not true. Gordo cares deeply for his father, Winston. Anything Winston wants, anything Winston thinks, anything Winston says, anything Winston believes, so does Gordo. You must be very careful, my friend. Winston and Fidel are not above killing those who get in their way of getting what they want, and they will certainly use Lonora to help them, and believe me when I tell you she will be all too happy to help, for Lonora is the evilest of all."

"She put you in the tree, did she not?" Goliath asked.

"She did, but not before I cast the reversal spell on the ruby stone that you found."

"What happened?"

"Lonora betrayed me. I thought I could help her unleash her powers for good, but she betrayed me and trapped me in the willow tree. When she did that, she lost some of her power and has been trapped in the house ever since. She is powerless outside of the house. I, however, gained the power that she lost and therefore have power everywhere I go." With that, Amethyst put the palms of her hands toward the entrance of the flower garden, and with the lavender glow of her hands, a huge hedge appeared and sealed the garden with Goliath and Amethyst inside.

"Oh, no! Amethyst, please! Please do not trap me in here!" Goliath ran up to the hedge in a panic.

"Calm yourself, my friend, I will let you out."

"Oh, good!" Goliath said with a sigh of relief.

"I will help you, Chloe, and Julia. I will help you three, but I must strengthen my powers back up and get a good handle on them. This will not be easy, my friend. Evil thrives when good men do nothing, you see. Good has been away from this house for a very long time and therefore evil has been thriving. There must be a battle, it is inevitable. I must be ready for it. I must be strong, focused, and well prepared, for I do not want any mishaps when the great battle begins."

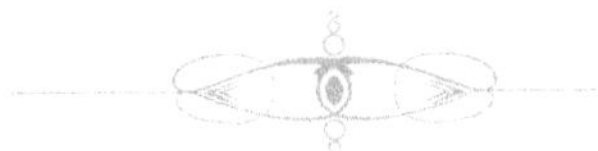

Chapter Fifteen

As Goliath talked to Amethyst in the flower garden, Chloe finished a beautiful painting.

"Wow! I have downright impressed myself!" Chloe said admiring her artwork.

"I told you! And why wouldn't you be talented? After all, your grandmother has been a household name for years." Julia smiled at her.

"I know, Nanny, but you are the famous artist, not me," Chloe said looking at all the paintings that Julia had found.

"Apparently, not in this world. Apparently, in this world, you are the famous artist. I am not surprised. Your talent must be genetic." Julia winked at Chloe.

"You are still a phenomenal artist! Look at that painting of Goliath! It looks just like him. What about Winston? Do you think he can paint too?"

"Absolutely not. These things are known to skip a generation." Julia and Chloe both laughed.

"Speaking of Winston, we better see what the rat and snake are up to. We can leave these down here to dry," Chloe told Julia, and they both went up the stairs and out of the studio. The two entered the kitchen just as Goliath ran in.

"Chloe! Julia! I am glad you both are here!" Goliath exclaimed out of breath.

"Goliath, what is wrong with you?" Chloe asked.

"I...must...catch...my...breath."

"Okay, well, while you catch your breath, Chloe and I are going to find Winston, Fidel, and Gordo," Julia said, as she and Chloe turned to leave.

"No! Wait!" Goliath exclaimed, then dropped his voice to a whisper. "I have something very important to show you outside, please come with me."

Julia and Chloe followed Goliath outside and walked down the beautiful flower-lined path.

"Look at all these beautiful flowers!" Julia exclaimed. "I did not know all this was back here."

"You ain't seen nothing yet," Goliath told Julia.

"You mean you haven't seen anything yet. We need to work on your grammar, Goliath," Julia told him, and Chloe chuckled. The laughter stopped, however, as they walked up to the hedge.

"What in the world?" Chloe asked.

"Amethyst! Amethyst! Let us in! I am here with Julia and Chloe," Goliath called quietly at the hedge. All of a sudden, a gust of wind blew, and lavender light shone brightly through the leaves and branches of the hedge as the hedge opened up. Julia and Chloe gasped, clutching each other's hands and looking at each other shocked at what they were witnessing.

"Come on! Hurry up, before we are seen!" Goliath told them as he walked through the opening in the hedge. Julia and Chloe obeyed and walked through. They stared in awe at the beautiful woman in the garden. "This is Amethyst," Goliath said with a smile. "She is going to help us."

As Goliath was introducing Chloe and Julia to the beautiful fairy in the flower garden, Lonora stood with Winston, Fidel, and Gordo in the pumpkin room.

"So we need to get to work on Chloe so we can get that money." Winston was sipping pumpkin juice.

"Something is wrong," Lonora said as she looked around the pumpkin room. Her hands began to tremble uncontrollably, and her eyes widened as she watched them.

"What is wrong with you?" Fidel asked.

"Something is not right." Lonora spun herself in a whisp of black smoke and turned herself into a bumblebee.

"What are you talking about?" Gordo said as he munched on pumpkin seeds. "Everything is fine."

"No, it is not. I feel something...disturbing." Lonora could feel as if something was off, some change was among them, but she could not explain it. "I better make sure that Chloe is still clueless about me, for I feel that something has changed. I can feel that something is not right."

"Well, shake it off, woman! We need to figure out what to do about Chloe," Fidel told Lonora.

"I think you are just being paranoid. Believe me, Chloe is clueless, Lonora. She would have warned us about you or attempted to get us all out of the house. She is not some brave heroine. Trust me, I know how to get what I want from her. I am going to begin by talking to her about justice, about doing what is right. You know Chloe, she is all about peace, harmony, always doing the right thing, and all that crap. It will be easy to convince her that giving everything to me, including the money and jewels, is the right thing to do," Winston said.

"Are you sure it will be as easy as you think?" Fidel asked.

"My father can do anything," Gordo answered.

"Chloe is so naive and ignorant, it will not be hard." Winston evilly grinned.

As Lonora, Gordo, Winston, and Fidel talked in the pumpkin room, Amethyst introduced herself to Chloe and Julia.

"Isn't she wonderful?" Goliath asked admiringly.

"I do not understand. Why do you think we are in so much danger? Why do you think there will be a battle? Why can't we just nip all this in the bud and take care of everything now?" Chloe asked.

"I could use a drink," Julia said as she sat on a bench.

"You cannot stay here, and as of right now, I am not strong enough to help you go back to where you belong. I have seen the hearts of those who are in the house with you," Amethyst answered Chloe.

"I see," Chloe stated. "I met with someone today who is also trying to get us back."

"You must be speaking of the professor," Amethyst said.

"Yes. How did you know that?" Chloe asked.

"Liam is a good man, and he will help but not without me," Amethyst responded. She then turned to a butterfly statue and pointed at it. With a lavender stream of light, the statue turned into a real butterfly. It floated in the air and then toward Amethyst. She lifted her hand slowly, and the butterfly landed gently in the palm of her hand, and she smiled sweetly before it flew away. Everyone watched her in awe.

"Wow!" Goliath whispered.

"But here is why I need to strengthen up," Amethyst said as she pointed to a gnome statue. The statue floated off the ground and shook. A few dark purple sparks ignited from the lavender light before it faded away, and the gnome statue fell back to the ground with a loud thud.

"Then we will leave you to it," Julia said standing up.

"Right, you stay here and work on your powers. The three of us will go on with everything as if nothing is going on. I am supposed to meet with Liam in a couple of days," Chloe said. The three walked to the hedge and then turned and looked at Amethyst expectantly.

"Stay safe, my friends," she said as she lifted her hands and opened the hedge. Goliath, Julia, and Chloe stepped through the hedge and watched as Amethyst closed it back up.

"I need a drink," Julia said again. Chloe and Goliath smiled at her as they all walked back toward the house.

As they walked back to the house, Winston spoke to Lonora who had transformed back into a sensual vixen.

"Now, you must keep an eye on Chloe. Watch her like a hawk," Winston said. Black smoke filled the room as Lonora transformed herself into a hawk. "Not literally," Winston told her, and she transformed back to herself. However, as she did, something warm, wet, and red dripped from her nose.

"What is that?" Gordo asked looking up at her nose.

"Is that blood?" Fidel asked.

"Impossible." Lonora reached up and touched her nose with a trembling hand. She looked at her fingertips covered in bright crimson red blood. With her other hand, she touched the tip of her nose with a trembling finger, and the bleeding stopped.

"Are you okay?" Winston asked.

"I am fine. I must leave you for now."

In a puff of black smoke, Lonora vanished. She reemerged at the end of the hall and looked out the window where she saw the familiar weeping willow.

"Amethyst," Lonora whispered, "are you right where I left you?" She stared at the tree for a bit, and her hands stopped trembling. "Of course you are." She smiled wickedly and then disappeared again in another poof of thick black smoke.

Chloe, Julia, and Goliath walked back into the house and into the kitchen. Chloe walked to the refrigerator and pulled out a pitcher of orange Kool-Aid. She reached in the cabinet and took out a brass goblet. She filled it with the bright orange sugar water and handed it to Julia.

"When I said I needed a drink, I was talking about something with a little more kick, like a martini," Julia told her.

"You are far too young for martinis. Drink this." Chloe smiled. "I need to figure out what to fix us for supper." Chloe opened the refrigerator and saw some chicken breasts. She took them out and then opened the freezer. She saw numerous bags of frozen vegetables and settled on the peas and carrots. She opened the cabinets until she found pots and pans. After taking out a large stock pot, she continued looking through the cupboards until she found a bag of egg noodles and some cream of chicken soup. She also found some chicken broth. "I will make a quick and easy chicken noodle soup," she said as Julia and Goliath watched her.

"What have you guys been up to?" Winston asked as he, Fidel, and Gordo entered the kitchen.

"I am about to cook some supper," Chloe answered.

"Thank God, I am starving," Gordo replied.

"What else is new," said Goliath.

"Goliath, be nice. What have you guys been up to?" Chloe asked as she started cooking.

"Oh, just exploring. Learning the ins and outs of this fascinating house," Winston answered.

"Oh, yeah? What is fascinating about it?" Julia asked as she sipped her Kool-Aid and then made a face. "Are you sure we cannot add some vodka or a nice gin to this sugar water?" Chloe smiled at her but did not answer.

"Oh, everything, really. The different rooms, the impressive size of the house. The phenomenal craftsmanship. Just everything about this house is fascinating," Fidel answered.

"Well, do not get too comfortable. We are going back to our world as soon as possible," Chloe said, cutting the chicken breast into cubes.

Soon supper was complete, and everyone sat and ate a comforting meal. After they ate, they all decided to go to bed and start again the next day. As Chloe and Goliath went into their new bedroom, Chloe looked at the painting. Goliath stared at it but did not get the same feeling he had before. Chloe looked at Goliath, and he looked back at her and shook his head. They both looked under the bed and saw nothing. They got into the bed and closed their eyes trying desperately to fall asleep, but neither one of them could. In fact, nobody in the house could sleep. Their minds were wandering all over different things, and it was a sleepless night for the group nonetheless.

As the sun rose, Goliath stretched every bone and muscle he had in his human body. "Chloe? Chloe, are you awake?" he whispered.

"Yes," Chloe answered. She sat up in the bed and smiled at Goliath. "I see you are still a human."

"Do not remind me," Goliath said sadly. "I did not sleep a wink last night. Normally, I would just play with my wonderful tail until I drifted off to sleep, but I do not have a tail anymore."

"You will again soon, I hope." Chloe smiled at Goliath and ran her fingers through his hair and gave him a scratch behind his ear.

"There's that magical power of yours." Goliath smiled. "How did you sleep?" Goliath asked Chloe as she got out of bed and put on a cotton robe.

"Not well, I am afraid. My mind would not stop."

"What does that mean?" Goliath asked.

"It means, um, that I had so many things running around in my brain that I could not relax enough to fall asleep."

"Oh, I understand that. That is what kept me up too. I was listening for things, you know."

"Yeah, Goliath, I know. Come on, let's go downstairs and start some coffee."

"You go. I think I am going to go outside and, you know, explore."

"Okay, just be safe," Chloe said to him as she exited the bedroom and went down to the kitchen. She was surprised to see Winston on the table with a steaming cup of coffee in front of him. "Well, good morning, Uncle Winston." Chloe smiled at him as she walked to the cupboard.

"Good morning, sweet niece," Winston said. "I made coffee."

"I see that. How did you accomplish such a feat?"

"It was not easy," Winston answered. "This body is very hard to get used to."

"I bet," Chloe said as she sat down. She glanced out the window and saw Goliath trotting toward the flower garden. "How did you sleep?" Chloe asked.

"Not good, not good at all. I feel so, you know, betrayed," Winston answered.

"Betrayed?" Chloe asked, confused, as she turned to face him.

"Wouldn't you be? Wouldn't you feel betrayed if you found out that your inheritance was being given to somebody else?"

"What makes you think that you are not getting your inheritance? What makes you think you are even entitled to an inheritance? I thought an inheritance was what someone left someone else at their own discretion. What is your obsession with an inheritance?" Chloe asked as she sat at the table with her coffee, clearly frustrated with his greed.

"I can read between the lines, Chloe, dear," Winston said as he sipped. "Do not fret, I obviously do not blame you. In fact, I believe that your heart is so good that you will make sure that I get exactly what I deserve."

"Uncle Winston"—Chloe looked down at him and smiled warmly—"I would not have it any other way."

"That is a relief." Winston put his paw on Chloe's hand. "So I can count on you then. I can count on you to do the right thing and give me my entire inheritance. You know, Mother being a famous artist, she is worth millions, and I am sincerely hoping I can count on you to relinquish it all to me." Winston was speaking in a hushed whisper.

"Uncle Winston, don't you think you are jumping the gun? I mean, Nanny is still alive and, well, is actually a very young girl right now."

"Chloe, we will be going back to our world, and when we do, I want to know that I can count on you to do the right thing. After all, since the death of my sister, your mother, I have been very good to you. I have tried to be a parental figure to you. I have given you love and support and compassion to the best of my ability. Mother had two children. My sister is gone, it is just me now, and it is my right to inherit everything. After all I have done for you, I would certainly expect you to do the right thing, Chloe. You know how much I love you. You know that I will always take care of you. Do the just thing. Give me what I deserve, ensure that I receive what is my right as Mother's only living son. Only living child, for that matter. Wouldn't you agree that I have been good to you?"

"Yes, Uncle Winston, you have. I promise you will get everything that you deserve. I just think you should live in the moment and worry about your inheritance when the time comes. I must get ready. I have an appointment in town at nine." Chloe stood up.

"Chloe?"

"Uncle Winston, when Nanny is gone, we will continue this discussion. Until then, let's just enjoy every moment we have, okay?" Chloe turned and walked out of the kitchen. As soon as she was gone, Lonora appeared, and Fidel came out from under the table.

"Did you hear her? I knew it! Stupid girl! She thinks I care so much about her. She thinks she is important to me." Winston grinned. "She is going to give it all to me."

"Yes, but not until Julia is gone, and with our luck, Julia is liable to outlive us all," Fidel responded.

"Not necessarily," Lonora said. "We could certainly make sure that Julia does not outlive anyone. We can simply speed things up a little, and nobody would ever find out that we did. The child cannot stop Chloe if she is dead." She looked at Winston, and they both laughed wickedly.

Chapter Sixteen

After Chloe met with Mr. Addlebock, she walked down the sidewalk dodging people who were hustling about and going on about their business. Chloe did not stand out as she was wearing the appropriate attire of cardigan, skirt, and black sandals. In fact, it seemed as if nobody noticed her at all, which made her feel comfortable and at ease. Chloe decided to stop at a little coffee shop. It was lunchtime, and her stomach was growling, telling her she was hungry. She walked into the coffee shop and was surprised to see Liam sitting at a table with a cup of soup and a sandwich in front of him, smiling and waving at her.

"Hello"—Chloe smiled and approached him—"I did not expect to see you here."

"Yes, this is one of my favorite places to have lunch. Won't you join me?" Liam gestured toward the chair across from him.

"How nice, thank you." Chloe smiled and sat down. A waitress approached and gave Chloe a menu. Chloe ordered a water and requested what Liam was having.

"So what brings you to town today?" Liam asked.

"I came to meet with Mr. Addlebock. I had some documents to sign."

"Ah. Mr. Addlebock is an excellent attorney, the best actually." At that time, Petunia walked up to them.

"Ms. Graham, what a surprise to see you here," she said with a smile. "Liam, how's the soup?"

"Delicious as always, Petunia," Liam answered.

"Hello, Ms. Picklepick." Chloe smiled at her. "I was in town meeting Mr. Addlebock and thought I would stop in here for a little lunch."

"Again, please call me Petunia. This place is definitely the best. I ordered a sandwich and a cup of soup to take back to the office with me, and I believe I see that it is ready. You two enjoy your lunch." Petunia walked toward the counter and picked up her soup and sandwich, and then left the coffee shop.

"I never asked you what your last name was," Liam said.

"No, I suppose you did not," Chloe said as the waitress put a sandwich and cup of soup in front of her, for which she smiled politely and thanked the waitress.

"You are Chloe Graham."

"That's right."

"Chloe Graham, the artist." Liam smiled from ear to ear.

"Apparently, I am." Chloe smiled as she sipped her soup. The warm, creamy tomato broth felt comforting, as it ran smoothly down her throat. Her senses awakened as the combination of basil and oregano hit her palate.

"I cannot believe this, I just cannot believe this." Liam sat back in his chair and continued to smile at Chloe in complete and utter admiration.

"What?"

"You are my favorite artist! Excuse me, I am a little starstruck. I have one of your paintings in my office!"

"The painting behind your desk," Chloe said taking a bite of her sandwich. It was just as delicious as the soup—a turkey sandwich on multigrain toast, with fresh, crispy lettuce and smooth, creamy avocado. The tangy fresh tomato dripped juice out from the edges of the toast, and Chloe dabbed her mouth with a napkin.

"Yes! You noticed it. Why did you not say anything?" Liam asked her and she shrugged.

"I guess I was preoccupied with finding out information on the vial."

"Yes, about that. I actually have some information for you."

"That was fast, that is great!" Chloe exclaimed, enjoying her lunch as it truly hit the spot. Liam was right about the food at this little hole-in-the-wall coffee shop for it was delicious.

"The name of the vial is Fawda Sufia."

"What?"

"Fawda Sufia. It is Arabic for 'mystic chaos,'" Liam answered as he finished his sandwich.

"Mystic chaos. That sounds about right." Chloe grinned as she took a drink of her ice water.

"The red ruby on the vial symbolizes chaos."

"Symbolizes chaos. The color red, you mean."

"Very good, I am impressed. You know Egyptian culture?" Liam grinned at Chloe.

"Do not be too impressed. I only know what red means because I saw it on Google. I saw that red symbolized chaos and disruption, which makes a whole lot of sense to me since that is what we are certainly in the middle of. A whole lot of chaos and disruption." Chloe finished her soup and sandwich and wiped her mouth with her napkin.

"I see, whatever would we do without the internet?"

"Look it up in books, like they did in the good old days," Chloe answered, and they both laughed. Chloe was enjoying her time with Liam, and likewise, Liam was enjoying his time with Chloe. There was definitely a spark and instant attraction between them.

"Yes, indeed. I also found, with my research, that the vial you need to go back to where you came from is called Ealim Mthali. It contains a blue sapphire, rather than a red ruby."

"Ealim Mthali?"

"Arabic for 'perfect world.' The blue stone, such as the sapphire, is very much loved by the Egyptians. Blue symbolizes the heavens, water which brings life, and things like that."

"It is a good thing you speak Arabic. Impressive," Chloe said before finishing her water.

"I am actually fluent in Arabic and Hebrew."

"Even more impressive." Chloe smiled.

"I am flattered you think so, Ms. Graham." Liam grinned and gazed at her adoringly.

"So where do we find this Ealim Mthali?" Chloe asked, shaking of the gaze and getting back to business.

"Ah, that is the thing. I have some leave time I need to take, and I thought I would take it to travel up to Autumleaf and visit my old professor and mentor, Dr. Waklilly."

"You think Dr. Waklilly will know where we can get this vial?" Chloe asked as the waitress brought the check.

"I think it is possible. He knows everything there is to know about such artifacts, so I am hoping that he knows where we can find the needed vial. Lunch is on me." Liam took the check.

"Thank you very much. Not only for lunch, but for believing me. I know that this must sound absolutely insane."

"You are very welcome. Would you like to accompany me to Autumleaf? Dr. Waklilly has a big enough house, we would have separate rooms, perfectly innocent, we would stay the night and come back the next day. It is about an eight-hour drive to Autumleaf. We would leave tomorrow morning around seven."

Chloe thought for a minute before answering. "Yes, I would like to accompany you. We desperately need this Ealim Mthali, and I do enjoy road trips."

While Chloe was having lunch with Liam, Lonora was meeting with Winston, Fidel, and Gordo in the garden room.

"I will be creating a toxin," Lonora said quietly.

"A toxin?" Gordo asked.

"Yes, a poisonous potion. This potion can be poured a little at a time into anything that Julia is ingesting," Lonora answered.

"Poison? Why can't I just force her to fall down the stairs?" Fidel asked. "I could wrap my sensuous body around her, wrap myself around her ankles, and oopsie daisy, down she goes falling to her not so tragic death."

"Or I could sneak into her room at night and place a pillow over her face. I could hold it down tight, and I will not let go until she stops kicking," Winston said with his hands clutched tightly as he illustrated his horrific statement.

"You cannot do that. You cannot do any of that," Lonora said quietly.

"Oh, I think I can," Winston retorted.

"I mean, you cannot do that and get away with it. It would be way too obvious, and Chloe would call pest control and have you both killed for killing Julia. No, the toxin will be the only untraceable way to do away with her."

"Excellent," Winston said slyly.

"How on earth will you be carrying a toxin around without being questioned about it?" Fidel asked. "You are a rat, not a kangaroo. How will you hide it? You do not have a pouch or pockets."

"I have thought of that too." Lonora smiled as she gently placed her hand on Winston's stomach. Black smoke wafted from Lonora's hand onto Winston's stomach and then engulfed him. Winston doubled over in excruciating pain.

"Ah! Oh!" Winston shrieked. Lonora smiled. "What is happening to me? Pain, lots of pain!" Winston was trying to catch his breath; the pain was unbearable.

"Stop! What are you doing to him?" Gordo exclaimed.

"You are killing him!" Fidel yelled. He and Gordo were panicked as they watched what they believed to be Lonora destroying Winston.

"Shh. You will see, pets," Lonora said quietly, "you will see that I truly am on the side of the wicked." Lonora watched as Winston wriggled and writhed in pain, black smoke still billowing from her hands. Fidel and Gordo watched too in horror. Lonora then started to close her fingers to make fists and as she did the smoke vanished.

Winston lay on the floor, breathless, moaning, and groaning. He blinked his beady eyes.

"Stand up, Winston," Lonora said.

"Would you look at that?" Winston stood up looking down at his stomach. He stuck his hand down into a pouch that Lonora had created upon him.

"Is that a pouch, like a kangaroo pouch?" Fidel asked.

"It is! It is!" Winston exclaimed.

"And it is deep. It is deep enough that you will be able to conceal a small ampoule of potion." Lonora smiled.

"Oh, Lonora! You are a piece of work, a real piece of work!" Fidel said with a smile. "We thought she was killing you!"

"So did I," Winston responded.

"She is wicked," Gordo said, and then turned his pig ears. "Someone is coming," Gordo whispered. With that, Lonora lifted her hands and vanished in a puff of smoke.

"What are you three up to?" Julia asked as she entered the garden room.

"Just talking," Fidel answered.

"I see. I was just wondering what you three were doing, since I really have not seen much of you," Julia told him.

"Yes, well, we have just been enjoying ourselves in these interesting rooms," Fidel replied.

"All right then. I am going to lay down and take a little nap. Chloe should be home any minute, if she wonders where I am, will you tell her?"

"Yes, of course," Fidel answered. Julia left the room.

"Whew! That was close!" Winston said. "Lonora! Lonora! The coast is clear," Winston called out, and Lonora reemerged.

"I will begin working on the toxin immediately."

"Yes, please do. The sooner the better. The quicker we can get Julia out of the way, the quicker we can get our hands on the money," Fidel replied. Lonora nodded and then vanished. Their plan would work beautifully for them. Julia knew that Fidel and Winston were sneaky, greedy, and hateful, but she had no idea just how dangerous they truly were.

Chapter Seventeen

Chloe walked through the front door of the house, humming to herself. She had a lovely lunch, and she enjoyed the company even more.

"I'm so happy you are home!" Goliath came running up to Chloe.

"Me too. What have you been up to today?" Chloe smiled.

"Oh, just spending some time with…" Goliath looked around and then whispered, "You know who."

"Ah, yes." Chloe grinned at her best friend.

"She is wonderful," Goliath whispered, and Chloe continued smiling at him as she walked into the kitchen. She got down a wine glass and poured herself a little wine from a pinot grigio bottle she found in the refrigerator. Goliath walked up to her and looked at her curiously.

"What are you looking at?" she asked.

"You, of course, you seem…happy." Goliath leaned in close to her and sniffed. "You smell happy." Goliath grinned at his girl, who simply shrugged off his suspicion. As they were talking, Julia came into the kitchen.

"You were gone a long time," Julia said. "Is everything okay?"

"Yes." Chloe moved over to the table with her glass. "I stopped at a coffee shop and had lunch while I was in town."

"Hmm, with whom?" Julia asked as she climbed onto the chair next to Chloe.

"What do you mean?"

"Chloe Elizabeth Graham, you blushed when you said you stopped for lunch. Now, why would you do that? I will tell you why, you had lunch with a man, did you not?"

"Oh, Nanny." Chloe looked down, for she could not seem to meet her grandmother's gaze.

"Chloe, I have known you since the day you were born. You cannot fool me. I have gazed upon your face your entire life, and even though you may not look the way you did a couple days ago, you still have the same expressions and features. Now, come on, tell me who you had lunch with."

"Well, it was not planned. I went to the coffee shop and Dr. Donnelson was there, Liam Donnelson, you know? He asked me to join him for lunch and so I did."

"Now, that is more like it. So tell me about this Dr. Donnelson."

"Well, I will, but first I need to go get the others," Chloe said standing up.

"They were in the garden room last I saw them." Julia smiled.

Chloe entered the garden room and saw Winston munching on an enormous radish.

"Chloe! When did you get back?" Winston asked.

"Just now. Will you three come downstairs to the kitchen please? We need to talk."

As Chloe walked back downstairs and into the kitchen, she caught Julia sipping the glass of wine Chloe had poured herself. "Nanny! You are too young for wine!" Chloe exclaimed, taking the glass from her. "I will fix you a glass of milk."

"Oh, all right!" Julia pouted and watched Chloe open the refrigerator and pull out a carton of chocolate milk. She poured it in a small glass.

"Here, chocolate milk." Chloe smiled as she put the glass in front of Julia.

"Oh, boy," Julia said sarcastically as she took the milk. Winston, Fidel, and Gordo joined Goliath, Chloe, and Julia in the kitchen.

"I had a very interesting day today," Chloe began, sitting down and taking a sip of her wine.

"Oh?" Winston was intrigued, hoping she was going to share some information that would be of some monetary gain for him.

"Yes, today I learned that the vial that Nanny gave me is called Fawda Sufia," Chloe began.

"Wow, is that some magical language?" Goliath asked.

"No, stupid. There's no such thing as a magical language. It is Chinese." Winston, confident in his intelligence, rolled his eyes at Goliath.

"Do not call me stupid! I could eat you for my supper, you stinking rat," Goliath hissed.

"Boys, boys, do not fight. It is not a magical language, Goliath, and it is not Chinese, Uncle Winston. It is Arabic. Arabic for 'mystic chaos,'" Chloe told them.

"I was unaware that you spoke Arabic," Julia said.

"Mystic chaos?" Fidel asked.

"Yes, mystic chaos, and I do not speak Arabic. Liam does," Chloe answered.

"Who is Liam?" Gordo asked.

"He is the professor at the university here who is helping us out of this mess. Anyway, we need to find the vial called Ealim Mthali."

"And what does that mean?" Winston asked.

"Ealim Mthali means 'perfect world' in Arabic. That vial looks just like the vial that Goliath accidentally broke except instead of a ruby it has a sapphire."

"Well, it sounds to me like you did have an interesting day." Julia smiled at Chloe.

"I did, indeed," Chloe responded with a smile as she took another sip of her wine.

"Okay, where is this Ealim Mthali?" Gordo asked.

"Well, that is the thing. Liam has invited me to join him in speaking to his mentor, a Dr. Waklilly. He lives in a town called Autumleaf, and according to Liam, this Dr. Waklilly knows everything there is to know about these types of things. So, that being said, I will be gone all day tomorrow and will be back home some time the day after."

"Um, Chloe…," Julia started.

"Nanny, do not worry, we will be staying in separate rooms. Autumleaf is an eight-hour drive from here. It would be ridiculous to drive back and forth in one day. We will leave early tomorrow morning, drive up there, meet with Dr. Waklilly, get some sleep, and head back here the next morning."

"Well, all right then. Sounds like you have it all worked out," Julia said as she finished her milk.

"Yes, ma'am. And I better go ahead and start packing since I will be leaving so early in the morning," Chloe said as she finished her dry, tangy beverage.

"I will go with you and help." Julia stood up, as did Goliath.

"Me too, me too," Goliath said, and he and Julia followed Chloe up to her room.

"Do you realize what this means?" Winston asked excitedly when he was sure Julia, Chloe, and Goliath were out of earshot.

"Yessss." Fidel smiled and slithered.

"What?" Gordo asked.

"Quick! To the bathroom!" Winston scurried off the table, and the three ran to the bathroom. "Lonora! Lonora!"

"I am here," said the mermaid swimming with the fish on the wall.

"How close are you to getting that potion made up?" Winston asked.

"Very," Lonora answered.

"Well, we need it by tomorrow morning!" Fidel exclaimed.

"Yes, indeed. Chloe is leaving town, and it will be the perfect time to use it," Winston said.

"I will have it for you by then."

"Excellent." Winston twisted his whiskers.

As the three sadistic creatures were in the bathroom with Lonora, Chloe was packing a bag talking to the two people in the world she trusted the most.

"Chloe, dear, I want to talk to you about this relationship you are developing with this Liam fellow," Julia said quietly.

"What relationship? There is no relationship. We are friends, that is all."

"You have feelings for him, Chloe," Goliath said. "We can tell, can't we, Nanny?"

"Yes, Goliath, that is right."

"Oh! You two!" Chloe blushed as the two of them continued. They were both right, of course. She was very attracted to Liam, and she thought he might be attracted to her as well.

"Chloe, it is not a good fit, honey. We do not belong here. This is his world, but it is not your world. If you fall in love with this man, if this man falls in love with you, honey, it will only end in heartache. Heartache for both of you." Julia looked seven, but her words were the words of a wise and mature woman. A woman who had done her very best to guide and advise Chloe her entire life.

"Yeah, what she said," Goliath chimed in as he lay belly down on the bed.

"I know." Chloe sighed. "He is really nice. He is friendly and handsome, and he is helping us."

"And he is becoming your hero," Julia said quietly.

"I guess." Chloe shrugged and sighed again as she sat on the bed between Goliath, who was still lying belly down, and Julia.

"I understand. I truly do. Your grandfather was the love of my life, and he was my hero. I have always prayed that you would find the kind of love that your grandfather and I had. I still pray that, but, Chloe, my sweet, this is not it. This cannot be it. This is a relationship that could not possibly end well. You are not a seventy-five-year-old woman, Chloe, and you do not belong in this world, and you will not be staying in this world, but he will. He will stay in this world when you, my dear, are long gone. I do not want to see you go through that heartache, and you do not want him to go through that heartache, do you?"

"No, of course not," Chloe whispered sadly.

"Just keep that in mind, please, and keep your feelings in check." Julia squeezed Chloe's hand, and Chloe smiled a small smile at her.

"Do not worry, Chloe. You will always have me," Goliath said as he sat up and wrapped his arm around Chloe's shoulders.

"And who could ask for a better companion." Julia smiled at Goliath and Chloe. Chloe chuckled.

Chapter Eighteen

The next morning, Winston and Fidel snuck into the music box room, leaving Gordo snoring on the floor of their bedroom. Winston tiptoed ever so slightly, and Fidel quietly slithered as they were trying to be as quiet as they could so as not to be caught by Chloe, Julia, or Goliath. The ballerina in the middle of the music box room stopped spinning suddenly and hopped off the pedestal when Winston carefully closed the door without making a sound. Winston and Fidel watched her gracefully dance toward them.

"Good morning," the ballerina said melodically. "I believe you are looking for this." She held out her ceramic hand, and in a puff of black smoke, she presented Winston with a light pink ampoule, no bigger than a teardrop.

"This is it, huh? It is not very big. Not very impressive at all. Is this really going to do the trick?" Winston looked at it.

"Quick, put it in your pouch, before we get caught," Fidel hissed.

"You will pop the little round tip off and pour the contents into whatever Julia is ingesting." The ballerina danced around the room before hopping back up on the pedestal.

"If Mother becomes ill, won't a doctor be able to help her?" Winston asked as he put the potion in his pouch.

"Slowly, oh, so slowly, she will grow weaker and weaker," the ballerina answered as she spun on her pedestal.

"Not too slowly, I hope," Fidel replied.

"You cannot rush these things. You cannot rush perfection, and believe me, this potion is perfect. Footsteps approach." The ballerina grew silent as she continued to slowly spin on the pedestal to the delicate waltz.

The door opened, and Winston and Fidel looked up to see Chloe standing at the door, looking quite lovely in a brown skirt, black sandals, bronze blouse, and black cardigan.

"I am off. I just wanted to say goodbye. What are you two up to in here?" Chloe asked.

"I am trying to teach my husband to dance," Winston answered, coming up with a lie quite quickly.

"Uncle Winston, Fidel is a snake. He has no feet."

"Nor does he have any rhythm, I am afraid." Winston laughed nervously.

"Okay. Please behave yourselves while I am gone," Chloe said suspiciously.

"Oh, Chloe! Of course we will, you silly girl. Everything will be just fine while you are away." Winston grinned at his niece. Chloe nodded and closed the door.

Chloe trotted down the stairs and saw Goliath and Julia waiting for her at the door.

"Be safe, sweetheart," Julia said as she hugged and kissed Chloe goodbye.

"I will."

"You do not have to worry about a thing, Chloe. I will take care of things while you are gone but come back as soon as you can. I miss you terribly when you are not home." Goliath hugged Chloe tightly.

"Thank you, Goliath, I appreciate you taking care of things while I am away. I will be home just as soon as possible, just make sure you do not eat Uncle Winston in my absence." Chloe smiled.

"Boy, she sure sucked the fun out of what we had planned, didn't she?" Julia joked. At that precise moment, there was a knock at the door. Chloe answered it and smiled when she saw Liam wearing a pair of black slacks, black shoes, and a dark purple button-down shirt.

"Good morning," Liam said with a smile when he saw Chloe. He was so attracted to her. He loved how her eyes sparkled, her complexion was stunning, and he would be more than happy to see her smile every day for the rest of his life.

"Good morning." Chloe smiled at him. He looked so handsome, and Chloe's heart fluttered when she saw him. It wasn't just his outer appearance that made him so attractive to her. He was so kind, and as Julia had pointed out earlier, he was becoming her hero.

"Oh, my," Julia said as she looked at the silver fox before her.

"Good morning to you, young lady. Who might you be?" Liam asked Julia.

"Oh, this is Julia, and this is Goliath," Chloe introduced them. "This is Liam."

"Nice to meet you," Goliath said. "Please make sure to take excellent care of Chloe. She is very important."

"Of course." Liam nodded.

"Let's get going," Chloe said. She turned to Julia and Goliath and gave them another hug and kiss goodbye.

"Do not forget what I told you," Julia whispered. Chloe smiled and nodded at her and then walked out the door.

Liam drove a black Dodge pickup truck. He opened the passenger side door for Chloe, and she hopped up into the seat. She thanked him and he smiled at her.

"I hope you drink coffee," Liam told Chloe as he got into the driver seat.

"Drink coffee? You could put it in an IV and hook it up to my arm." Chloe laughed as did Liam.

"Me too. This is for you, then." Liam handed Chloe a paper cup filled with rich, dark coffee for which she thanked him.

As Chloe and Liam pulled away, Winston scurried down the stairs and saw Julia and Goliath standing at the door.

"I miss her already," Goliath said sadly.

"Do not fret, handsome cat, she will be home soon enough." Julia smiled warmly at Goliath and squeezed his hand.

"Thank you for that, Nanny. Thank you for calling me a handsome cat." Goliath smiled at her, and she nodded.

"Good morning, Mother," Winston said, and Goliath hissed at him.

"Winston," Julia said.

"Can I fix you a cup of coffee?" Winston asked.

"If you are able."

Winston scurried to the kitchen and up on the counter. He quickly grabbed a coffee cup and secretly opened the ampoule and poured the contents—a clear, tasteless, and odorless serum—in the bottom of the cup before Julia and Goliath could enter the kitchen. He then tipped the coffee pot, and though he was able to pour coffee in the cup, he got the majority of it on the counter, and it dripped off the edge of the counter and onto the floor. He smelled it, and all he smelled was coffee. He smiled wickedly as he called to Julia.

"Mother, your coffee is ready," Winston hollered.

"Thank you, Winston," Julia said as she reached for the cup on the counter. "Winston! Did you make this mess?"

"This body limits my abilities, Mother," Winston answered.

"Well, I am confident that you have the ability to clean it up," she responded as she sipped the coffee. "This is delightful, thank you." She took her coffee to the table, and she sat down next to Goliath. Winston began cleaning up the mess he had made, but he made sure to watch his mother out of the corner of his eye. His heart fluttered with excitement. He did not understand it really. He knew what he was doing was wrong. He knew that what he was doing was beyond wrong—actually, it was complete evil. He knew he was poisoning his own mother, yet for some reason, he was downright giddy, and he was truly having a hard time containing it.

Meanwhile, Chloe was looking out the window while Liam drove down the highway. It was another cloudy day, and there was a heavy fog resting on the fields that they passed by.

"So, Ms. Graham, when did you start painting?" Liam asked.

"I do not know, really. In my world, I am not a painter, I am a writer."

"A writer?" Liam asked. He was so anxious to get to know the beautiful woman that was sitting next to him.

"Yes, sir. I did not know that I could paint until I came here. It sounds crazy, I know, but it is what it is." Chloe smiled a small smile.

"Not too crazy, really. Writing is creative and artistic, painting is creative and artistic. It makes sense that you would be creative and artistic no matter what world you are in."

"Yeah, I guess so." Chloe smiled at him. She was enjoying talking to him, but she kept thinking of the conversation that she had with her grandmother just the night before.

"You are obviously a very creative and artistic person."

"And you, what made you want to be a professor of Egyptian culture?" Chloe asked.

"I have always been fascinated in other cultures, not just Egyptian culture, but every culture. I love learning about how other people live. I also have always loved sharing that knowledge with others. That is why I went into teaching. I used to teach high school."

"Oh? What made you stop?"

"The students, honestly. They just do not respect teachers like they used to. You know, like you and I did in our day. Young people today have no respect for authority. That is what is wrong with the world today, you know? Young people today are being taught that they do not have to respect anyone. They are not being taught to be kind. They are being taught to be selfish. They are being taught that they are entitled to everything and that it is okay to be hateful, rude, and disobedient. They are not being taught to work for what they want, they are being taught that they are entitled to what they want. You know, I heard a man yesterday speaking so rudely to someone, and as I thought about how disrespectful he was being, I heard him say that respect is earned. I did not grow up that way. I grew up being told you respect others regardless. You respect people's space, their property, their feelings, but disrespect, however, disrespect is earned. I would never speak with such foul language or disrespectful language as the way I was talked to as a teacher."

"So who is to blame for that? Parents?" Chloe asked.

"Society. It is not just the parents, it is society as a whole. It takes a village, as they say."

"So you thought you would wait until they matured a little bit?" Chloe asked.

"That and my class is an elective. The students I have choose to take my class. It is better, I must say. When they enter college, they are considered adults, and I do not have to hold their hands to get assignments done. I am not expected to beg them to do their work or grade them on a curve to make sure they pass the class. I tell them what their assignment is, and they either do it or they do not." Liam stopped and noticed Chloe watching him as he spoke. "I am talking too much, aren't I?"

"No, not at all. I agree with what you're saying about young people not respecting their elders anymore. You know, when I was growing up, I firmly believed that my teachers had permission to swat me if I misbehaved. The kids I went to school with did too. I do not ever remember any of my classmates swearing at the teachers or being disrespectful to the teachers. I mean, if a teacher told you to do something, you did it. If a teacher told you to stop doing something, you stopped." Actually, what Liam was saying made him even more attractive to Chloe. She was excited that they had the same view and opinions.

"Yeah, exactly. It is not like that today." Liam shook his head. "So enough about that. I should get off my soapbox. So what do you write? Books? Do you write for a newspaper? Do you write for a magazine?"

"I write books. A little of every genre. I write children's stories. I also write some poetry, and I have been working on the third book in my adult murder mystery series. I have not made it to the top, but one day I hope to be a bestselling author."

"That is interesting." Liam smiled as he got to know a woman who he believed to be quite fascinating.

While Chloe and Liam were getting to know each other, Goliath was in the flower garden visiting with Amethyst. Amethyst was practicing her magic. She was creating beautiful things. Flowers, butterflies, songbirds, and she had magically made the fountain flow with water that changed colors. Hues of pink, blue, lavender, green, and yellow water flowed freely.

"Amethyst, you are wonderful." Goliath applauded her.

"Not yet, but I will be." Amethyst smiled. "How are things in the house?"

"Fine, I suppose. Julia is painting. She painted a picture of me, of what I used to look like, and it was truly a masterpiece. She is famous, you know? In our world, she is a famous artist. Her work is in art books and everything. Chloe is very proud of her."

"Sounds like you are too." Amethyst had such a warm smile. She was a warm being. A being that you wanted to be around. She made Goliath feel calm, peaceful, and happy.

"Julia has always been very good to me. When I was a cat, she would let me lay on her lap, and she would scratch behind my ears and rub my back. She would let me take naps on her bed. She has just always been good to me. I love her." Goliath smiled at the memory.

"And Chloe? What has she been doing?" Amethyst asked.

"Chloe is on a little trip right now. She has gone with her friend Liam to Autumleaf to talk to someone about a vial that can send us back to our world."

"Ah, yes, the Ealim Mthali."

"Yeah, that is it. You know of it?"

"It is thought to be a myth, but I think you, Chloe, and Julia are proof that it is not."

"Amethyst?"

"Yes, my friend."

"Can you send us back? Can you turn us back into who we used to be? Can you turn me back into the most gorgeous cat in the whole world?"

"I am afraid not. I am not powerful enough for that. Not yet anyway."

"Oh," Goliath said sadly, "I understand, I suppose. I wish I knew more about such things."

"You wish you knew what?"

"Fawda something, and something Mthali."

"The vials are supposed to be just a story. Would you like to hear the story?" Amethyst sat next to Goliath on the bench, as he nodded happily. "A long time ago, a very long time ago, I had a very good friend. He was a pixie, and his name was Bartholomew." Amethyst's eyes grew sad as her mind wandered into the past, and she remembered her best friend. "Now, you see, back in those days, pixies and fairies were not to be friends. They were not allowed to be friends."

"Not allowed to be friends? Why not?" Goliath could not fathom such a thing.

"Pixies are different than fairies, you see? Pixies are small, mischievous, and ornery. They also have short tempers, and they can come off quite abrupt and rude. Fairies, on the other hand, are supposed to be gentle, kind, and peaceful. Fairies are not supposed to play tricks on people or cause any mischief. So as you can understand now, fairies and pixies are very different creatures, and because we are different, we were not allowed to be friends," Amethyst answered.

"I don't understand, Amethyst. Chloe says that our differences make us special and that we should always get to know someone before we decide not to like them. She says something about a book and a cover, I do not really remember exactly what she says."

"We fear what we do not understand, friend. Fairies do not understand the antics of a pixie any more than a pixie understands the fairy. Therefore it was a rule that pixies and fairies stay away from each other. They were absolutely not to be friends. Spending time with each other, socializing with each other was considered a terrible betrayal and was actually punishable by death."

"By death? My goodness! That is terrible." Goliath was shocked.

"Anyway, Bartholomew and I tried to keep our friendship a secret, but Lonora found out about it."

"And she put you in that tree." Goliath was listening intently.

"Yes, she put me in the tree, after starting a battle between the fairies and the pixies. Bartholomew was executed, and there was a battle between the fairies and the pixies. The pixies won the battle."

"Executed? What is executed?"

Tears touched Amethysts eyes as she said the words, "My friend, Bartholomew, was killed. Before he was killed, however, there was a rumor that he created two potions. One potion would bring heroes here to bring peace to Snickerdoodle. Once peace had been achieved, the other potion would send the heroes back to their home, wherever that may be."

"Amethyst, do you know where the potion to send us back is?" Goliath asked.

"No. I did not believe that Bartholomew created such potions. I thought it was simply a rumor, nothing more, just a myth."

"Just like fairies."

"Yes, Goliath, just like fairies. But as you now know, fairies are not myths, and neither are those potions."

Chapter Nineteen

Goliath walked back into the house. He decided it would be best not to tell anyone what Amethyst told him. He did not want anyone to be mad at her, for she was a gentle and loving soul, and Goliath really liked her. Goliath noticed, as he walked into the kitchen, that Julia was nowhere to be seen, so he trotted down to the studio, assuming she was still painting. He gasped, however, when he saw her small form slumped lifelessly forward, her head resting on the table in front of an easel and next to a palette of oil paints. Her eyes were closed, and Goliath was panicked.

"Julia!" Goliath hollered. He could not move; the fear and dread had paralyzed him in the entrance of the studio. Winston and Fidel were keeping fairly close to Julia, though out of sight. They heard Goliath holler and quickly ran to see the alleged fruits of their labor. They rushed up behind him.

"What in the world is wrong with you?" Winston asked. Goliath could not speak, he just pointed toward the small child, his hand trembling uncontrollably. "Oh, no! Call 911!" Winston exclaimed, as he rushed to Julia's side. He scurried up the table as Goliath watched in horror, still unable to move. Winston put his paw on Julia's shoulder. "She is breathing," Winston stated, somewhat disappointedly. At that instant, Julia opened her eyes. "You are okay?" Winston asked.

"What?" Julia asked.

"Oh my gosh, Julia! I thought you were dead!" Goliath hurried up beside her.

"Ssso did we." Fidel slithered.

"Oh, my! I must have dozed off. How very peculiar," Julia said as she rubbed her eyes and yawned.

"Dozed off? You mean, you were just sleeping?" Winston asked.

"I do that all the time," Goliath said, relieved that Julia was fine and had just taken a little nap. Chloe would never forgive him if anything happened to Julia while she was in Autumnleaf with Liam Donnelson.

"Yes, well, I am fine. Just sleepy, is all," Julia said as she stood from her chair and stretched her tiny body. "I think I may go to my room and lie down. I do not know what has come over me, I am just so tired all of a sudden."

"Yes, Mother, you do that. Go take a nap in your room," Winston said as he watched her carefully. Why was she not dead? Did the potion not work? If she went to lie down and doze off again, would she never awaken?

Chloe and Liam were enjoying their time together. They pulled up in front of a large Victorian-style home. It was white with olive green shutters, a maroon shingled roof, and large white pillars garnished the front. There was a huge wraparound porch with two porch swings and three rocking chairs all made of redwood. The home sat on six acres of beautiful land. Rolling hills of bright green clover, a completely different atmosphere than that of Snickerdoodle. There were pecan trees, precisely landscaped along with apple, pear, and peach trees.

"Wow! This place is beautiful!" Chloe exclaimed as she hopped out of Liam's pickup truck. She took a deep, refreshing breath as the smell of the trees and the crisp, fresh air filled her lungs.

"Yeah, it is really nice," Liam said with a smile as Chloe looked around and smiling as she admired the beauty that surrounded her.

"Liam! Liam!" A plump bald man stepped out of the front door, walking with a cane, dressed in khaki pants, and a black button-down shirt. "There you are!"

"Hello, Honoraville!" Liam smiled and gestured for Chloe to follow him toward the front porch.

"Liam, it is so good to see you! Look at you! You look great! And this lovely lady must be Chloe Graham," Dr. Honoraville Waklilly extended his hand to Chloe, and when she reached out to shake it, he brought it up to his lips and kissed it gently. "You are as lovely as Liam said you were."

"Thank you!" Chloe said and smiled warmly.

"She is a gem. And look at you, Honoraville! You look wonderful! You do not look a day over sixty!" Liam said as he and Honoraville embraced in a tight hug.

"Oh, right. Come on in here, I will fix us some drinks," Honoraville said as he turned to walk into the house. As they entered, Chloe could not help but notice the beautiful craftsmanship of the home with breathtaking, ivory-painted crown molding throughout the house and seventeen-foot ceilings. The home was decorated with Victorian furniture, and the walls were painted in muted colors, making the house look even more massive yet welcoming.

"Your home is beautiful, Dr. Waklilly," Chloe said as she followed Liam and Honoraville into the parlor.

"Dear, you may call me Honoraville." He sat down and poured himself a scotch, then poured one for Liam and one for Chloe. He handed them their glasses, sat back in his chair, and took a long sip.

"I see you are still a scotch man." Liam smiled.

"Liam, I will be ninety-six in a couple of months, and I will tell you, I credit my longevity to a few scotches a day."

Liam and Chloe laughed at the man. He was a very happy man, it seemed, friendly and kind, and Chloe was looking forward to knowing him.

"So Liam tells me you are interested in the legend of Fawda Sufia," Honoraville said to Chloe.

"Yes, sir, very interested."

"It is an interesting legend, really. You see, the legend states that Fawda Sufia is one of two vials containing a potion created by a very powerful pixie. Fawda Sufia is a vial laced with gold and has a red ruby in the center and small red stones throughout. Fawda Sufia, as I am sure Liam told you, means 'mystic chaos' in Arabic. Anyway, the myth states that anyone who comes into contact with the potion inside the vial will be transformed and transported to another dimension. The pixie did, however, create a counter potion and put the potion in Ealim Mthali. That, again I am sure Liam told you, means 'perfect world' in Arabic. Ealim Mthali is a vial nearly identical to Fawda Sufia, except it has a sapphire stone and blue stones rather than the ruby and red stones. The potion in Ealim Mthali, when poured on the person that was affected by Fawda Sufia, will return to how things were. It is a myth though." Honoraville finished his scotch and poured him another.

"What was the name of the pixie that created the potions?" Chloe asked. She immediately thought of the persnickety little pixie floating around in the bubble while she and her trusted companions were exploring Snickerdoodle.

"I do not think I ever heard the name, honey, it was just a powerful pixie. The pixies of Snickerdoodle have grown significantly in population since the civil war."

"Civil war? Civil war, as in Yankees and Confederates?" Chloe asked.

"I am sorry, what? Whatever are you talking about?" Honoraville looked at Chloe like she had two heads.

"It is nothing, I am sorry, continue." Chloe took a long drink, for obviously Dr. Waklilly was speaking of a different civil war and not the American Civil War.

"Yes, the war between the pixies and fairies. The pixies won, of course, wiping out all the fairies and all but three unicorns. A sad tale, really. Fairies were warmer and kinder than the obnoxious pixie."

"Where can we get the Ealim Mthali, if we wanted one?" Liam asked.

"Well, you cannot, my boy. It does not exist. It is just folklore, it is simply a bedtime story. It is simply a myth told around campfires," Honoraville answered.

"So you are saying that both the Fawda Sufia and the Ealim Mthali are nonexistent," Chloe said as she sipped her scotch.

"Of course."

"But, sir, they are not," Chloe said to the man.

"Oh, my dear lady, you cannot tell me that you believe in such things as magical potions and mystic vials." Honoraville laughed.

"I did not, but I certainly do now," Chloe stated plainly. "I did not believe in unicorns and pixies and fairies, but I do now."

"You are pulling my leg." Honoraville laughed even harder. "She has got an excellent sense of humor, Liam, an excellent sense of humor," he said as Chloe stared at him.

"She does, Honoraville, she certainly does." Liam laughed and took Chloe's hand. Chloe looked at Liam, and he gave her a look, a specific look, a look that Chloe understood immediately. If this man heard her story, he would think her absolutely insane.

"It just so happens, I have a book here that I think you would enjoy. The story of Fawda Sufia and Ealim Mthali are in it, along with a very brief summary of the great fair-pixie war. I pulled it off my bookshelf when Liam told me you both were coming to discuss the legend." Honoraville picked up a small book off his end table and handed it to Chloe. "Here, my dear. Take it."

"Thanks, Honoraville! I appreciate that!" Liam smiled at his friend and drank his scotch.

"Yes, thank you so much!" Chloe said as she took the book and then took another sip.

"My pleasure. Now, let me show you where your rooms are." Honoraville stood up and Liam and Chloe followed. The doctor led them up a glamourous winding wooden staircase garnished with a wrought-iron handrail and into a long hallway. A crystal chandelier hung from the center of the ceiling. "Ms. Graham, this is your room." Honoraville opened the door to a large suite with a silver king-sized canopy bed covered in a satin lavender comforter. The bed had four pillows, two large lavender and two white throw pillows. There was a large fireplace in the room with an intricately carved mantle and a beautiful wood dressing table. The floor was a light hardwood and looked freshly polished.

"This is beautiful," Chloe said, "thank you."

"Of course, dear. Liam, this way." Honoraville led Liam down the hall to the next door and opened it. Liam's room also had freshly polished light hardwood flooring, and the bed in his room was a king-sized sleigh bed. It was covered in a royal blue comforter and had two large royal blue pillows and two black throw pillows. Just like in Chloe's room, Liam's room had a fireplace with a stunning, gleaming marble mantle, but no dressing table, rather it had a chest of drawers containing six drawers, two small at top and four larger drawers remaining.

"Thank you, Honoraville." Liam smiled at his friend.

"Think nothing of it. I will let the two of you get settled and changed for dinner. See you down below in an hour." Honoraville left the two to get settled in their rooms.

A couple hours later, Liam was dressed in a dapper black tuxedo, and Chloe was wearing a lovely silver evening gown that shimmered in the light. They sat together on a small love seat in front of a roaring fire, sipping chamomile tea after their succulent prime rib dinner. Honoraville had gone to bed, and Liam and Chloe were simply making small talk. They talked about how delicious the meal was and how nice Honoraville was. They talked about how beautiful his home was and how he and Liam had been friends for so long. They would watch each other as they each spoke, almost longingly. The chemistry between them, the attraction, was beyond obvious. Though they were from different worlds, they had so much in common, and Liam could not help but feel as if something special was happening between them. He felt like he could talk to her this way for the rest of his life. He was falling in love with her.

"Please understand, Chloe, I only looked at you the way I did because—"

"You did not want the good doctor to think me absolutely bonkers," Chloe finished Liam's sentence. "I completely understand." She sipped her tea.

"Right! Exactly! I had hoped I did not offend you." Liam smiled at her.

"No, of course not." Chloe smiled back. Liam gently put his arm across Chloe's shoulders and pulled him to her. He could not resist, he just could not. They had something special. They had a connection. They were meant to meet, and they were meant to be in this moment together. Liam knew it with every bit of his heart. He kissed her softly, gently, and she returned the kiss. The kiss then grew from soft and gentle to deep and passionate. Liam pulled Chloe closer, tighter. His heart pounding, his mind racing, all he could hope was that she wanted him as much as he wanted her. He knew he was falling deeply in love with this woman, though they hadn't known each other but for a few days. Chloe melted in his arms as the sensual kiss took her breath away, her heart fluttered, her stomach flipped, every part of her body tingled, and then reality struck her, and she pushed him away. She pushed him away slowly but pushed him away she did and caught her breath.

"I am sorry," Liam said as he blushed. Had he misread the entire situation? Did he have feelings for a woman who had no feelings for him? He was beyond embarrassed.

"Liam, I feel very strongly for you. I do. But this…us…this just cannot happen. As much as I would like it to. I would love nothing more than to explore this relationship that you and I have. To see how far we could take it. We are obviously very attracted to each other, and I think that if it was a different time, you and I would have something so spectacular, something so wonderful, something so magical. Unfortunately, we just can't. Unfortunately, you and I are from two different worlds and a relationship between you and I could not possibly have a happy ending," Chloe said quietly. Surprisingly to her, she was fighting back tears as she felt her heart breaking a little as she spoke.

"Of course, I understand that. I am so sorry. I guess I just got caught up in a moment, you know. I feel strongly for you too. I like you a lot, and with the fire, the atmosphere, I just…I am sorry. You are right, we could not possibly have a meaningful relationship."

"We could be friends, very good friends." Chloe smiled a small smile at him, even though her heart was breaking a little. She enjoyed kissing him and would love to keep kissing him, for she was consumed with passion and emotions she had never before been consumed with; but her mind went to what her grandmother had told her, and she could not bear to break Liam's heart. She certainly did not want to be heartbroken either and she had such strong feelings for him.

"Yes. I would like that very much." Liam smiled at her. "Well, it is late, and we have a long drive tomorrow. I am going to bed." Liam stood up and Chloe stood up with him. They both walked up the stairs, said goodnight, and went into their own rooms.

Chloe slipped into her soft cotton nightgown. A part of her was a little sad, disappointed even. She got into the bed, pulled the covers up around her, and opened the book that Honoraville had given her. She flipped through the pages until she found the story she wanted to read.

The Great Battle of the Pixies and Fairies

Many moons ago, when this world was populated by pixie and fairy alike, there was a great battle. This battle was the demise of the fairy.

The fairies were kind and generous and wanted to live harmoniously with the pixies, but the pixies were mischievous, cold, and greedy. The pixies wanted complete control of Oddity's lands and resources. That is except for Bartholomew Jahosephat. Bartholomew cared deeply for a very specific fairy. The most powerful fairy of them all. They were the best of friends. They kept their friendship a secret, however, because pixies and fairies were so different in what they believed to be appropriate behavior.

As most fairies were, this fairy that Bartholomew had befriended was good, kind, beautiful, and gentle. Her magic was a thing of beauty. That all changed though when she was betrayed. There was another fairy, you see. The other fairy had an evil streak. She was greedy, cruel, and dark. The beautiful fairy, however, being the kind soul that she was, felt pity for the dark fairy and was determined to find the good in her. For years it seemed to have worked. For

> the beautiful fairy's kindness seemed to melt the dark fairy's cold heart, and the dark fairy was showing love and admiration to the beautiful fairy. The beautiful fairy was teaching the dark fairy how to strengthen her powers so that she could do good things with them. Some things just remain the same, unfortunately, and the dark fairy betrayed Bartholomew and the beautiful fairy. The dark fairy told the leader of the pixies about Bartholomew's friendship, and he was executed.
>
> The beautiful fairy, enraged and devastated, led the fairies into war atop unicorns with golden horns. The dark fairy, however, used her powers against the other fairies, not only betraying the beautiful fairy but all the fairies. The fairies were completely obliterated as were all but three mare unicorns.
>
> Legend states that Bartholomew, fearing the repercussions should his friendship with the beautiful fairy be revealed, created two vials of potions. The first was Fawda Sufia and the second Ealim Mthali. Fawda Sufia was created to bring forth brave heroes to right the wrong of the dark fairy and the pixies, and when the time is right, Ealim Mthali will be used to send the saviors back to where they originated.

Chloe closed the book and thought of what she just read. According to the book, all the fairies were gone. Chloe knew this to be untrue because Amethyst was currently in her new backyard. Was she the beautiful fairy that the pixie died for? Did Amethyst know about these vials? If so, surely she knew where the potion was to get them back home, and why would she keep that information from them? Was she trapping them in this world? If so, Amethyst was not the good fairy Chloe thought she was, and they may be in more danger than they thought.

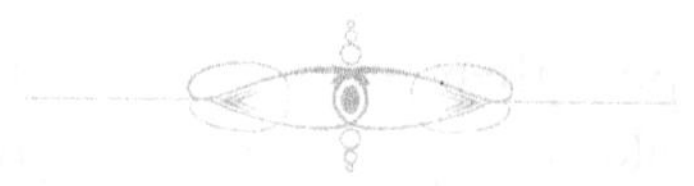

Chapter Twenty

The drive back home was quiet as Chloe looked out the window while Liam drove. She had so much on her mind. She went to Autumnleaf to get answers, instead she just had more questions.

"You are awful quiet," Liam said to her.

"It is not a myth," Chloe replied quietly.

"I know."

"Where is it? We know that Ealim Mthali exists, so where is it?" Chloe turned her face away from the window and looked at Liam, who was watching the road before him.

"I do not know. Maybe it is in Egypt. You said your grandmother got the Fawda Sufia in Egypt, perhaps Ealim Mthali is there too."

"That is another thing, why Egypt? Why would some pixie create these magical potions, put them in vials, and send them to Egypt? Why would he not keep them here, in this world?"

"I cannot answer that, Chloe," Liam told her.

"Neither can I, but I might know somebody who can."

"Oh? Who?" Liam was curious.

"It doesn't matter." Chloe went back to looking out the window.

Liam reached over and held her hand, his touch warm and immediately giving Chloe butterflies in her stomach. "If this person can't, I can make some calls to shops in Egypt. Where did your grandmother obtain the Fawda Sufia? What city? What was the name of the shop?"

"I do not know," Chloe said feeling silly for not finding that information out in the first place and desperately trying to ignore the feeling of butterflies in her stomach.

"Find that out. That would be a good lead on finding the vial to send you home." Liam squeezed Chloe's hand before placing it gently back on the steering wheel.

"Thank you, Liam." Chloe smiled a small smile at him.

"That's what friends are for," Liam replied. Those words stung. They really stung them both.

As Liam and Chloe were driving home, Winston was continuing with his devious plan, though he was getting frustrated that things were not progressing faster than they were. He had wanted to pour the poison in his mother's coffee one time and be done with it.

"Lonora!" Winston called out from the pumpkin room. "Lonora! Where are you? You have some serious explaining to do!"

"Whatever do you mean?" A face emerged in a giant pumpkin seed hanging from the dome-shaped ceiling.

"Your potion did not work," Winston told the seed. "All it did was put her to sleep. I did not expect a sleeping potion. You said we were going to kill her with this poison, but all it did was assist her in taking a nice, refreshing nap!" Winston was angry and felt like Lonora was playing him for a fool.

"I told you," said the pumpkin seed, "you cannot rush perfection. I told you this would happen slowly. Meet me in the garden room in half an hour and I will give you another ampoule." With that, the face inside the pumpkin seed vanished, and Winston let out a long sigh.

Julia sat at the kitchen table with a cup of coffee in front of her. She felt more awake now and chalked it up to all the rest she got the day before.

"What time do you think Chloe will be back?" Goliath asked sitting next to Julia.

"I do not know, dear, but I am sure it will be some time this afternoon."

"What do you think of this Liam fellow?"

"I think he is a very nice man." Julia smiled at Goliath.

"I do too, and I think he really likes Chloe."

"Who wouldn't?" Julia asked.

"A rat and a snake," Goliath commented.

"Well, their distaste for Chloe is not because of who she is, it is because of what she is, Goliath," Julia informed him.

"What does that mean?" Goliath asked curiously.

"She is my granddaughter, and they know that I love her like a daughter. She is my world, and they cannot stand it. It is more about jealousy. Jealousy and greed, of course. They want it all, they do not want to share, and I believe it infuriates them that they will have to."

"Oh, that makes sense," Goliath replied thoughtfully.

As Julia and Goliath visited in the kitchen, Winston waited impatiently in the garden room. He was wringing his hands and pacing back and forth. Suddenly a granite statue in the garden caught his attention. It was a statue of a little girl smelling a flower. He had not noticed it before, perhaps because it was not the statue that caught his attention but the red glow around it. Winston inched himself, carefully, toward the statue. His nose twitched as he got closer and closer. The statue started to tremble, and then miraculously, the little girl turned her face away from the flower and toward him, causing him to jump back.

"Lonora?" Winston asked.

"Here." The flower that the little girl was holding turned into a tiny ampoule, identical to the ampoule that Lonora had given him before. "As you requested."

"Will this do it? Will this do the trick?" Winston asked, taking the ampoule and putting it in his pouch.

The statue bent over and plucked a fuzzy dandelion from the earth. She placed it to her lips and puckered up as if to blow it, but then the dandelion turned to granite and, being held by the granite girl, became just another garden ornament.

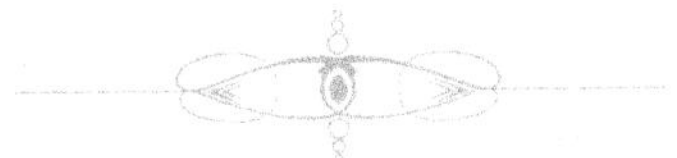

Chapter Twenty-One

Chloe walked through the front door feeling mentally, emotionally, and physically drained. As she put her overnight bag down, she smiled at Goliath.

"You are home!" Goliath trotted up to her and gave her a tight hug. He was so happy to see his favorite girl.

"I am. Where is Nanny?" Chloe asked.

"Here I am," Julia answered as she walked up to Chloe. She had dark circles under her young eyes, which Chloe could not help but notice.

"You look tired, Nanny, are you okay?"

"I just seem to be worn out for some reason. Doesn't make sense, really, I slept almost all day yesterday, and I felt rested up this morning, but now I am sleepy again."

"Strange." Chloe was concerned.

"I had my coffee this morning, feeling just fine, then I had a bowl of oatmeal and I started getting tired again, probably just the change of things, you know how it is," Julia told Chloe, seeing the worry in her eyes.

"I think it is because of the nasty raisins Winston put in your bowl for you. He got them out of a jar, and they did not smell very good to me," Goliath chimed in, and Julia and Chloe both smiled at him. Goliath never liked the smell of raisins as a cat, so it seemed logical that as a human he still would not. As a cat, he would give them a sniff then snort and gag as he would saunter away from them. The raisins Winston gave Julia for her oatmeal that morning were nasty, however, as they were tainted with a toxin created by Lonora.

"I have some stuff to talk to you all about. Where is Uncle Winston, Fidel, and Gordo?"

"I will go find them," Goliath ran off to find the rat, snake, and pig.

"You look tired yourself, my sweet." Julia took Chloe's hand and led her to the kitchen where they both sat down at the table.

"I had a restless night," Chloe replied, and Julia cocked an eyebrow. "Nothing like that, Nanny. Have you talked to Amethyst?" she asked quietly in case anyone was within earshot.

"No, but Goliath has been spending quite a bit of time with her," Julia answered.

"Where in Egypt did you get the vial? What city? What was the name of the shop?"

"I honestly do not remember the name of the shop, but it was in Giza," Julia answered. "I do remember that the shop was very small. In fact, that is what enticed me to look inside. I also remember that the little shopkeeper was an older gentleman. He owned the shop, and your grandfather and I had a very nice chat with him. I remember him to be quite interesting," she told Chloe.

"Interesting? How so?"

"Oh, just the way he found the items in the shop. The shop was not like a store you would go to here, it did not have clothes or bulk items. What this fellow did was go out and about and find artifacts left behind by the people who had long ago passed on."

"Like a gravedigger?" Chloe asked.

"No, honey, no. Remember when you were a little girl, and you would go out and dig through the dirt and find arrowheads and old bottles and jars? He would do the same. He would find old clay pots, broken rock with hieroglyphics on it, even broken pieces of things that he would put together, old stones and jewels which he would take and make into jewelry, things like that."

"Things like old vials with potions in them," Chloe told her.

"I suppose so," Julia replied thoughtfully. "I am sure that the man did not realize that the potion was in the vial when he found it though. He probably tried to open it just like you did and could not.

He probably thought it was pretty and would be a nice addition to his little shop."

"I am sure you are right," Chloe said, squeezing her grandmother's tiny hand as everyone else came into the kitchen.

"How was your trip?" Winston asked as he scampered up onto the table.

"It was fine. As you all know, we were transformed and transported by a potion in a vial called Fawda Sufia. The potion we need to go back is Ealim Mthali. Now, according to legend, the potions were created by a pixie named Bartholomew. I do not know how Fawda Sufia got in Giza, Egypt, but it did, and now we need to find the Ealim Mthali. I do not know if it is in Giza too, or if it is somewhere here in Snickerdoodle, but finding it is imperative," Chloe reported to the group.

"Sssso this doctor you went and saw told you about a pixie that made potions? Ssssilly, isn't it? Ssssounds like this doctor is a quack to me," Fidel hissed.

"You cannot honestly say that after everything we have gone through these past few days that anything surprises you, Fidel. Of course the potions were created by a pixie. We have seen pixies, we know they are floating around in bubbles all around town," Julia replied.

"Right, and I want to find that little crabby pixie that stuck her pointed tongue out at me. Perhaps, that pixie knows where the potion is. My biggest question is how the potions got to Egypt in the first place. Nowhere did I see that the pixie sent the potions there nor why," said Chloe.

"Does it really matter?" Gordo asked. "I mean, really, all that matters is that we find it and go home. I am tired of eating healthy garden food and pumpkin. I want steak. I want pizza, meatloaf, mashed potatoes, a nice juicy porkchop…" Gordo stopped as he realized he was currently a pig.

"How very cannibalistic," Julia joked.

"Look, you guys, Liam and I are going to continue searching for the vial, but if you guys see anything or hear anything, it would be helpful. No matter how insignificant you think it may be, it could be exactly what we need to find it, okay?" Chloe was not smiling, she was not grinning; she was stern and very serious. Everyone nodded, and Winston, Fidel, and Gordo left the kitchen, and once they were gone, Chloe turned her attention to Goliath who had been sitting quietly, listening to every word that was being said.

"Goliath, I hear you have been spending some quality time with our friend Amethyst," Chloe said quietly, almost a whisper in case of prying ears.

"Yes, yes, I have," Goliath answered.

"What have you learned from her?"

"I learned about the pixie you talked about."

"The snappy one in the bubble?" Julia asked as she yawned and put her head down on her arms, which she crossed on the table in front of her.

"Nanny, are you okay?" Chloe asked.

"Oh, I am fine, just sleepy. I am listening to you both, do not mind me," Julia answered tiredly. Julia's eyes were open yet heavy.

"No, not that one, Bartholomew. He was Amethyst's best friend, and that evil witch betrayed them, and he was killed. She said she thought the potions were just something called a rumor," Goliath told the lovely ladies what he knew.

"So she has no idea where the vials are?" Chloe questioned.

"No, but she is working on her powers so she can help us get back home."

"Okay, Goliath, I would like for you see how she is coming along with that," Chloe told him, and he got up and went outside to visit with his new friend.

"I do not know, Nanny, I just do not know. Amethyst may not be the good fairy we think she is," Chloe told Julia as she watched Goliath walk down the flowered pathway.

While Chloe spoke to Julia and Goliath, Fidel, Gordo, and Winston sat in the garden room.

"What a joke," Winston said as he sat in the dirt and snacked on a chunk of radish.

"What do you mean, Dad?" Gordo asked as he rooted around in the soil.

"Hello, pets," a bumblebee replied as it buzzed around the evildoers.

"Hello, Lonora," Fidel responded.

"Lonora, I am going to need another ampoule," Winston said, and then explained himself to Gordo, "What I mean, son, is pixies creating potions and shipping them off to faraway lands is absolutely preposterous. Fawda Sufia, Ealim Mthali indeed."

At the naming of the potions, Lonora transformed from the bumblebee to her human form. "What did you just say? How do you know of Fawda Sufia? Where did you hear that from?" She seemed quite disturbed.

"Fawda Sufia is the potion that sent us here, do you know of it?" Winston asked.

"I do, I disposed of it," Lonora said thoughtfully.

"Apparently not, because here we are, trapped in a weird house in repulsive bodies," Winston replied frustrated.

"Winston, speak for yourself, I happen to like my long, sleek form. I think it fits me just fine," replied Fidel.

"A pixie, an annoying little twit of a pixie, created the potion you're speaking of. He had intended to hide it, but I, the phenomenal spy that I am, caught him. I wrapped my perfect fingers around his bony little neck and squeezed until he dropped the vial in my hand. I simply used my powers to get rid of it, I caused it to vanish." Lonora was confused as to how this potion reemerged, and what was this Ealim Mthali Winston spoke of? She knew nothing about such a potion. Fawda Sufia was the only potion she saw Bartholomew make, so what was the other potion Winston was speaking of?

"You did a terrible job disposing of it, Lonora. It ended up in Giza, Egypt. You know, I am starting to think you are not nearly as powerful as you think you are. You could not dispose of a pixie potion, and this toxin you have allegedly concocted is not working either," Winston told her. Furious with the comments, Lonora's eyes filled with a bright, glowing amber flame, and she lifted her left hand toward Winston, which caused him to begin rising from the ground, dropping his radish chunk, legs dangling. He was gasping for air as his throat was closing up.

"Careful, friend, I could snap your neck without even touching you. I could easily kill you, and I will if you do not watch your attitude." Lonora looked so evil, so dark, as Winston's eyes grew bigger and bigger, nearly bugging out of his head.

"Lonora, please!" Fidel shrieked, and she released Winston, who fell to the ground coughing and desperately trying to regain the oxygen Lonora had cut off from his rat body.

"A warning, friends, a serious warning. Do not cross me." And with that, Lonora raised her hands, palms inward, and disappeared in a puff of black smoke.

Chapter Twenty-Two

"I am afraid that Goliath is being fooled by Amethyst. He thinks she is the best thing since catnip," Chloe told Julia. "I am going to go talk to her." She stood up to leave, as did Julia, yawning and stretching.

"Okay, let's go," she said.

"Let's? What is this 'let's' business? You are not going," Chloe told her matter-of-factly.

"Oh, yes, I am!" Julia exclaimed. "You are certainly not going into that garden alone with what may be an evil and extremely dangerous being! She could turn you into something unnatural!"

"And you are going to protect me?"

"Of course!" Julia said walking toward the door.

"Really, Nanny? In your three-foot body with your angelic face, how in the name of all that is holy do you think you are going to protect me?" Chloe asked her as she crossed her arms in front of herself.

"Good point, I will take a weapon." Julia started rummaging through drawers, inspecting things she would find and putting them back until she stumbled upon a tiny can of WD-40. "Ah! This will do it. If she tries any funny business, I will spray her with this. I will mace her with it!"

"Great, you will turn her into one big grease spot." Chloe smiled at her grandmother, who ignored the sarcastic comment, and they walked out the door, hand in hand, down the aromatic floral path.

Upstairs, Winston was watching the two walk down the pathway and toward a hedge. "Going for a little walk, I suppose," he said to himself as he observed.

"Here you are," Lonora snuck up behind Winston, making him jump nearly out of his skin.

"You surprised me," he told her.

"Surprised or frightened?" Lonora asked.

"Frightened, I suppose," he answered.

"Good, you should be frightened, I like frightened."

"I am so very sorry, Lonora, so sorry," Winston said to her. "I am just impatient, I guess. It will not happen again. I will never question you again. I swear it." He quivered inside. He used to think of Lonora as an ally, but after the incident in the garden room, he saw her more now as what she truly was—complete and absolute evil. She frightened him to his core as he now knew she could kill him at any given moment, and it seemed she would have no reservations in doing so.

"How delightfully refreshing." Lonora grinned at him before evaporating in a wisp of smoke.

Goliath, Julia, and Chloe came back into the house. Julia and Chloe were somewhat disappointed that they received no new information from Amethyst, just information that they already knew. Winston was waiting, perched on the table, with a steaming cup in front of him.

"I fixed you a cup of coffee, Mother, you look beat," he told Julia.

"How thoughtful, Winston, I cannot help but wonder why," she asked.

"I do not know why you look so tired either," Winston answered defensively. "How am I supposed to know that? I do not know how you are sleeping as we all suffer through this devastating predicament that we have found ourselves in."

"I mean, why are you being so thoughtful, it is really not like you," she responded.

"No need to be so defensive, Uncle Winston, it is a valid question." Chloe went to the coffee pot and poured herself a cup just as there was a knock on the front door of the house. The four in the kitchen looked at each other surprised. Chloe opened the door to find Liam standing on the stoop.

"Hi," he said, "may I come in?"

Chloe opened the door all the way and motioned for Liam to enter, who politely smiled and nodded at the group watching him. "What brings you over?" Chloe asked.

"I have not been able to stop thinking of you," Liam smiled gently at Chloe.

"Oh, my!" exclaimed Julia.

"I mean, your dilemma, I have not been able to stop thinking about the crisis at hand, that is all I meant." Liam cleared his throat and smiled, just as warmly, at Julia.

"Come, sit, have a cup of coffee with us," Julia responded, and Liam obeyed as he took a seat between Goliath and Julia. Liam eyed the rat on the table.

"Is that—"

"That is my Uncle Winston," Chloe interrupted Liam. "He was transformed into a rat, his husband a snake, and his son a pig. Dilemma might be an understatement, but crisis hits the nail on the head." Chloe handed him a steaming cup and sat across from him at the table with her own.

"Ah, I see," Liam said, taking a sip from the cup.

"Do I disgust you, sir?" Winston asked.

"You are a rat, Winston, you disgust everyone," Julia answered before Liam could.

"Well, you do not disgust me, Winston. As a matter of fact, you make me hungry. I for one think you look quite tasty," Goliath chimed in, leaning closer to the whiskered creature, who immediately jumped off the table and scurried up the stairs while Chloe and Julia chuckled.

"Goliath here was my cat," Chloe explained.

"I was the most handsome and bravest cat in all the world," Goliath told Liam.

"Snake and pig, huh?" Liam asked.

"Yep, not too far a stretch if you knew how they behaved as humans," Julia answered.

"Truer words were never spoken." Chloe smiled. "What did you want to discuss?" she asked, drinking her coffee.

"Did you find out where Fawda Sufia was purchased?" he asked.

"Giza," Julia answered, "I bought the vial in a little shop in Giza. I told Chloe all about it when she got home."

"According to Nanny, the owner of the shop would find abandoned artifacts, fix them up, clean them up, or whatever, and sell them in his little shop, but she cannot remember the name of the shop," Chloe stated.

"Well, that gives me a location anyway, and it helps knowing that it was a little shop and not a type of chain or big store." Liam continued drinking his coffee. "I will start making calls."

"I am going to get online on the laptop Nanny found and look around too. When all else fails, check Amazon." Chloe laughed at her own joke, but Liam was confused for he had never heard of such a thing.

"Amazon?"

"Never mind," Chloe answered, and Liam finished his coffee.

"I better get going," Liam said as he stood up.

"Stay for supper," Goliath told him. "Chloe is an excellent cook, and she makes delicious meals."

"I was thinking of making Salisbury steak tonight with some hamburger I found," she said.

"That does sound delicious, but I better get to researching where to find the Ealim Mthali," Liam responded as he walked to the door. The truth was, he wanted nothing more than to stay and have supper with them. He wanted to spend all his time with Chloe, but he knew he could not do that. They had decided to be nothing more than friends, and though it shattered his heart, he would do everything in his power to just be a friend. He had even considered not looking for the vial to send Chloe back, but then realized the longer she's here, the stronger his feelings for her would become. No, it was best to find the Ealim Mthali and send her home as soon as possible. To see her gone would break his heart, but the closer they got, and the stronger the feelings, the more unbearable her leaving would be. The three said goodbye to Liam, and Chloe sighed as she closed the door behind him.

"I like him," Goliath told her.

"So do I, he has been very helpful and kind, he is a good friend," Chloe told Goliath.

"Friend?" Julia asked.

"Yes, Nanny, we decided last night that given the current circumstances, we would remain very good friends and nothing more. Hungry?"

"I could eat," answered Julia.

Chloe busied herself making a delightful meal, which the family ate happily and then went to bed, but for Chloe, it was simply just another sleepless night, for her mind was completely cluttered with thoughts of the vial. Thoughts of where the vial could possibly be and whether or not they would ever find it. Her thoughts then drifted to Liam, and if they never found Ealim Mthali, would that be such a terrible thing? Who cared if Winston stayed a rat, Fidel was always a snake, and Gordo was indeed a pig? If they stayed in this world, Julia would get to be a child again, but even better, knowing what she knows as an adult, and thus not making any mistakes she may have made in the past, and perhaps Chloe and Liam were meant to be together. Perhaps they were not meant to find the vial, for perhaps they were where they were always supposed to be in the first place.

Chapter Twenty-Three

The next morning, Chloe woke up early as usual. She quietly walked out of the bathroom and tiptoed down the stairs, so as not to disturb anyone. She went into the kitchen and started the coffee pot. Chloe yawned as she waited patiently for the coffee to finish brewing and then poured herself a steaming cup. She slipped outside and stood in the back of the house.

As Chloe took a long sip of her rich, dark, bold brew, she stared at Amethyst's hedge. *Swoosh! Swoosh!* Chloe heard the song of enormous wings flapping as the palomino unicorn flew straight up from behind the hedge and out of the garden. She watched the unicorn in awe, when she saw something in her peripheral vision. The black-and-white unicorn was walking through her yard munching on the grass. Chloe smiled brightly and walked slowly toward the unicorn with her hand extended. The animal smelled her hand and neighed happily. Chloe slowly put her hand up and ran her fingers through its long, flowing mane. The unicorn allowed Chloe to run her hand down her neck and then down the rest of her body.

"You are an incredible creature," Chloe whispered. The unicorn extended her wings, causing Chloe to take a step back, and the breathtaking unicorn lifted off. Chloe watched in wonder, as it flew effortlessly away.

"Hey!" Goliath exclaimed, walking up behind Chloe leading her to jump.

"Hey," Chloe responded.

"I thought I would go see Amethyst for a while," he told her.

"Okay, is Nanny up?" she asked him.

"Yes, ma'am, she is at the table having coffee."

"Enjoy your visit," Chloe told Goliath and then turned and went back into the house. She did not want to share with anyone the magical moment she had just experienced. She wanted to keep that to herself. Chloe walked into the kitchen and sat with Julia. As the two drank coffee and visited with each other at the kitchen table, Winston entered.

"Good morning, all," Winston said as he sauntered into the kitchen, followed by his devious partners.

"Morning," Chloe replied.

"Coffee?" Winston asked and both Julia and Chloe raised their cups, indicating that they already had some. "How about some breakfast? Oatmeal?"

"No, thank you. Chloe, would you like some oatmeal, dear?" Julia asked.

"No, thanks, but I might whip up some muffins, how does that sound?" Chloe stood up and walked to a cabinet where she pulled down a glass mixing bowl.

"Wonderful!" Gordo exclaimed as drool edged out his mouth.

Chloe hustled around the kitchen getting flour and sugar, eggs, and milk. She found cabinets containing jars of spices and pulled out cinnamon, nutmeg, and cloves. Chloe quickly whipped up the muffin batter and poured it into a muffin tin. She turned her back to Winston who was watching her carefully as she put the milk and eggs back in the refrigerator, and as her back was turned, and neither she nor Julia were paying a bit of attention, Winston pulled the newest ampoule given to him by Lonora out of his pouch quickly and discreetly pouring the contents in one of the filled muffin cups, noting which one he poured the poison in so that the only one ingesting it would be Julia. Chloe tossed the muffins into the oven, and they all waited as the aroma filled the kitchen.

"Hmm, very good, Chloe," Julia said as she ate the muffin that Winston assured she would get, and he watched her devilishly as she ate it.

"Not bad, huh?" Chloe responded just as Goliath walked through the backdoor and into the kitchen.

"Something smells wonderful, I could smell it all the way outside," he said.

"Muffin?" Julia handed him a muffin, and Goliath took it, devoured it, and then took another.

"What do you ladies have planned for today?" Fidel asked.

"I am going to do some online shopping, sort of. I am going to browse Egyptian artifact stores and see if I can find the Ealim Mthali," Chloe answered.

"I might paint. I have been so tired lately, I have not finished the last painting I started." Julia stood up and then immediately sat back down. "On second thought, I might go back to bed. I am feeling quite dizzy and lightheaded all of a sudden."

"Are you okay?" Chloe asked extremely concerned.

"Just need to rest, I suppose. I may look like a young girl, but I fear my mind and body have not changed a bit."

"I do not remember you being this tired and feeling this way before, Nanny. Are you sure you are all right?"

"Of course, I am. I do not feel sick, I just feel drained. I will go lie down and take a little nap and then I will paint." Julia smiled and slowly walked into her room. She climbed into the bed, covered herself up, and fell into a deep sleep.

"Do you all think she is all right?" Chloe asked the remaining family members who were still in the kitchen.

"Oh, she is fine," Fidel answered.

"Yes, remember she is really eighty-four years old, Chloe, she just needs to rest. This whole ordeal has taken a lot out of all of us," Winston chimed in. Chloe thought about that and accepted it as she went upstairs to change out of her pajamas and into some clothes. Goliath went into Julia's room to check on her.

"I saw what you did, Winston," Fidel whispered to the rat. "How sneaky of you."

"This is it, this has to be the final dose. Perhaps Mother won't wake up at all from this nap," Winston evilly grinned.

Chloe came back down into the kitchen to find it empty. She looked out the window and saw Goliath walking toward the hedge, checking behind him periodically to make sure he was not being followed. She took out the laptop and started searching for Ealim Mthali. She, unfortunately, found absolutely nothing. Julia, fully clothed in a broomstick skirt, T-shirt, and cardigan, staggered into the kitchen as Goliath trotted into the kitchen.

"Liam is coming up the walk," Goliath said. Chloe quickly walked away from the laptop and to the front door, opening it before Liam had a chance to knock.

"What a pleasant surprise." Chloe smiled, and her heart fluttered at the sight of him.

"I was wondering if you would accompany me into town today. I have had no luck with the shops I have called in Giza, and I thought maybe we should check some of the antique shops here in Snickerdoodle," Liam responded and returned the smile.

"That sounds like a brilliant plan to me," Julia stated.

"Why don't you join us, Nanny? The fresh air may do you good. Perhaps a stroll around town would make you feel better," Chloe said.

"Perhaps you are right, sweetheart, let's go."

"Me too?" Goliath asked.

"Of course, Goliath," Chloe said, "you too."

"Oh, boy, an outing!" Goliath exclaimed as they joined Liam outside and walked together down the walkway, through the gate, and down the sidewalk to town.

As the four walked down the sidewalk, Chloe could not help but look for the snippy little pixie that was so agitated by her. Chloe did not find the pixie, but the pixie found her and buzzed up to her, not in a bubble this time.

"Hey, you!" the pixie said to Chloe flying right up in her face. "Remember me?"

"I do, actually," Chloe answered, "I have been wanting to talk to you—"

The pixie interrupted, "Yeah, well, I have been wanting to talk to you too, sorry for sticking my tongue out at you. The elders told me I must apologize to you, and so I have, and that is that." The pixie turned to fly away.

"Apology accepted, I suppose. Where are you off to in such a hurry?" Chloe asked, and the tiny thing turned, clearly offended by the question.

"None of your beeswax."

"I am Chloe."

"I do not care."

"Excuse me," Liam said to the persnickety creature, "my friend here is trying to be polite, the least you could do is give her your name. A proper introduction is all that is being requested here."

"Wintzella, my name is Wintzella," she answered. "Now if you do not mind…"

"Wintzella, do you know of Bartholomew?" Chloe asked and that stopped Wintzella in her tracks.

"We pixies do not speak of him. He disgraced the entire pixie race. Befriending a fairy, the nerve! We showed him, though, we ended him. We ended him and the weakling fairies."

"Boy, you sure are a mean little thing, aren't you," Julia said.

"Do you know of the potion Bartholomew created, Ealim Mthali?" Chloe continued with her questions.

"Oh, poppycock, there is no such thing. That is just a story someone made up. Now really, you have really wasted enough of my time, good day to you." And with that, Wintzella fluttered away.

"Gee whiz." Julia shook her head.

Liam opened the door to a small antique shop, and a jingling bell announced the arrival of Goliath, Chloe, Julia, and Liam. The shop smelled of citrus and sage, and the walls were lined with antique clocks, candlesticks, and porcelain dishes. As the group walked around the shop, inspecting the various items, a tall, lanky man with blond hair and bright blue eyes approached them. He was wearing a bright red button-down shirt and black slacks and had a ring on every finger. The watch he wore sparkled as if made of diamonds.

"May I help you?" he asked.

"We are just looking, thank you," Liam answered. They all inspected and admired everything on the shelves. They would pick them up, turn them around, even give things a little shake as the storekeeper watched them closely.

"Chloe, I am not feeling so well." Julia walked up to Chloe and took her hand while she looked carefully at an antique cuckoo clock.

"We better get you home," Chloe told her as she signaled to Liam and Goliath, who were looking at artifacts locked tightly in a glass display case. Goliath opened and held the door for the squad as they stepped outside. Petunia was walking down the busy sidewalk handing out flyers to the people she passed by.

"Ms. Graham!" she hollered and caught everyone's attention. She rushed up to Chloe and handed her the flyer. "Liam, how are you? Here, I hope to see you all tomorrow night at the bazaar," she told them as Liam and Chloe looked at the flyer she handed them. It read:

> Bazaar!
> Come one, come all to the 125th annual Snickerdoodle Bazaar!
> Food, rides, and vendors galore!
> Friday night, starting at 6:00 p.m.

"The bazaar! Is it already that time of year again?" Liam asked, more to himself than anyone in particular.

"Bazaar?" Goliath asked.

"It is a community gathering. Everyone really comes out for it. It is always fun, and there is always live music, delicious food, rides, and the vendors really are spectacular," Liam answered.

"Chloe?" Julia seemed to be trying to catch her breath. "I feel so…so…," Julia started and then collapsed in Chloe's arms.

Chapter Twenty-Four

Four humans and three animals surrounded Julia's bed, all watching her closely as her tiny form moved up and down with every breath she took. Liam and Goliath were standing at the foot of the bed, while Chloe was sitting to the left of Julia and holding her hand. A doctor was to the right of Julia listening to her heartbeat with his shiny stethoscope. Winston, Fidel, and Gordo quietly sat on the floor. The doctor was not surprised at all to see the animals in the room with Julia, for it was quite common for pets to be everywhere that their human companions were. He would, however, have been shocked to hear them speak, and for that reason, the creatures did not speak a word.

"Exhaustion," the doctor said. "She is not running a fever, and she does not seem to be overly dehydrated."

"What do we need to do?" Chloe asked with worried tears in her eyes.

"There is really nothing that can be done, miss. Plenty of rest, fluids to keep her hydrated, but that is it," he answered as he took the stethoscope out of his ears and placed it back in his bag. Julia opened her eyes and squeezed Chloe's hand.

"I am fine, just very sleepy," Julia told Chloe as Chloe squeezed Julia's tiny hand, returning the loving gesture.

"Then we will get out of your room and let you rest." Chloe stood up and kissed Julia's forehead and then turning to the door, sniffling as she held in the tears that were so close to pouring out. Liam and Goliath followed closely, and then Winston, Fidel, and Gordo joined. The six of them stood silently in the hallway outside the door, until the doctor emerged.

"That is it," he told them.

"Thanks, Doc," Liam said, extending his hand for a firm shake.

"My pleasure, let me know immediately if anything changes. It is strange for such a small child to be so worn out, but I honestly do not see any other ailment."

"Yes, sir, thank you so much for coming so quickly," Chloe said quietly, almost a whisper. The friendly doctor nodded and with that showed himself out of the only gray house in Snickerdoodle.

"Exhaustion?" Winston asked in disbelief.

"Well, you all have been through a lot," Liam said looking down at the rat.

"I am thankful it is exhaustion, my worst nightmare is losing the woman I love most in this world," Chloe replied wiping her eyes, for she could no longer fight back the tears of fear and concern. Liam wrapped his arms around her in a gentle hug, doing his best to comfort her. Her love for Julia was undeniable, and his heart ached to see her heart ache.

"Exhaustion?" Winston asked again and the group looked at him. "I just cannot believe that. Exhaustion!" Winston was very shocked indeed. In fact, he was holding in more than disbelief—he was holding in complete outrage.

"Chloe, would you like to go with me to the bazaar tomorrow night?" Liam asked. "I know it is kind of short notice, but vendors come from around the world to the Snickerdoodle bazaar. We may find something useful."

"I would, but I should probably stay here with Nanny," Chloe answered.

"You go," Goliath chimed in, "I will stay with her. I will take real good care of her."

"I don't know. I do not feel comfortable leaving her."

"She needs rest, so she is going to be doing a lot of ssssleeping. What could you possssibly do?" Fidel hissed.

"I could make sure she eats and stays hydrated. I could make sure she has plenty of fluids," Chloe answered.

"We will do that. You go and let us take care of her," Winston insisted.

"Well..."

"I won't let anything happen, Chloe," Goliath interrupted.

"I just..."

"Getting us back home is our top priority, getting us back home is what Mother needs right now, Chloe," Winston told her.

"All right, Liam, I will go with you tomorrow night, and hopefully, we will find what we so desperately need right now." Though Chloe accepted the invitation, she was not a hundred-percent sure she was making the right decision. She knew Goliath would do everything in his power to take care of Julia, but she did not trust the rat nor the snake. The pig would do whatever was asked of him, which made him a dangerous creature as well.

"Then I will pick you up around five thirty?"

"I will be ready." And with that, Liam smiled and said farewell. As he walked out the door, the remaining family members scattered. Chloe and Goliath to the kitchen, Fidel to the music box room in hopes of visiting with Lonora, Gordo to the garden room for something to eat, and Winston went to the pumpkin room to throw an absolute fit.

As he entered the pumpkin room, he muttered to himself, "I should have smothered her with a pillow when I had the chance to, or had Fidel cause her to fall down the stairs. Exhaustion!" Winston paced back and forth wringing his hands. "Unbelievable! Exhaustion! That witch has fooled us all, she has no intention of helping us." Winston was infuriated. Alone in the pumpkin room, his anger was free to come out. He picked up a fallen pumpkin seed from the floor and screamed in outrage as he threw it across the room. He then picked up a handful of pumpkin goo and threw it clear to the other side, where it hit the wall with a splat. He screamed one final time as he reared back and kicked the spongy pumpkin wall as hard as his rat strength could muster, and to his surprise, a piece of the wall flipped open, revealing a hidden room. Winston looked around, paranoid that he would be caught pitching his two-year-old childlike tantrum, then curiosity got the better of him as he carefully entered the room. He stepped forward and saw a winding staircase made of stone going downward. As he took another step, the piece of wall he had inadvertently opened flipped closed. Feeling he was trapped, he spun around in a panic and pushed the brick wall that was an entrance only seconds ago. He pushed and pushed at the wall to no avail. He looked around, breathing heavily, and saw burning torches were hung along the brick wall, evenly spaced and illuminating the staircase. Winston took each step, one at a time, slowly and carefully, desperately hoping that he would find a way out, until he found himself at the bottom of the stairs.

"Well, well, well, what have we here?" Winston asked himself.

Chapter Twenty-Five

Winston's feeling of panic was immediately replaced with awe. A massive dark laboratory was before him. Little red fireflies were floating effortlessly in the air, their red beacons so different from the white beacons of the fireflies in Alabama. They were everywhere, filling the room with flecks of red glittery light. The brick walls were lined with shelves that held all sorts of interesting things. Beakers, test tubes, goblets, books, and vials filled with extremely odd ingredients. Winston hopped off the bottom step and tried to capture a firefly. A pastime he enjoyed as a child, but as an adult, he just admired the pretty little insects from his porch. To his dismay, the red sparkle was too elusive, and he was unable to get a hold of it. He continued to explore the enormous lab he found himself in. He looked at the shelves to his right and picked up a golden goblet, and to his surprise the shelves moved and rearranged themselves.

"Oh, my!" Winston exclaimed. He looked closely at the shelves to find the shelf the goblet was on so that he could put it back exactly where he had found it. Thankfully, the half-inch-thick dust on the shelves revealed exactly where the goblet had been. He gently placed the goblet back on the shelf and the shelves moved again. Winston watched wide-eyed and fascinated with the magic of this place. He looked over other shelves and took a book. Once again, the shelves rearranged, but this time, he was too occupied with what he saw in the dusty, thick hardcover book to pay much attention to the movement of the shelves. It was full of recipes for potions. He studied the shelves and put the book back. He then moved over to another set of shelves. He picked up a vial and read the label.

"Frog eyes?" Winston put it back and grabbed another, all the while the shelves continued to move completely on their own. "Eye of newt, that is typical," he said reading the calligraphy on the vial and gingerly placing it back with the label facing forward so that Lonora would not know that he had been in there touching her things, for he knew this had to be her laboratory. He picked up one more ingredient. "Opossum tongue? Gross!" Winston went to put it back, quite disgusted, but when he did, he accidently knocked a couple test tubes off the shelf. He quickly put the opossum tongue back on the shelf and caught the test tubes before they could fall on the floor and shatter, with lightning-speed reflexes. He put them back on the shelf as well, though he was not exactly sure they were in the right place. Winston continued to investigate the room. He noticed an enormous cast-iron cauldron nestled in a fireplace, brewing and bubbling over a small fire with a hot pink mixture, though the smoke that emerged from the mixture was lime green. Winston was mesmerized as he stared at it for a brief second. He continued to search for a way out of this mad scientist's paradise when he noticed a large wicker basket on a big round table made of steel. He scampered up the table and saw that the basket was full of the ampoules that Lonora had been giving him one at a time. There had to be thousands of ampoules in the basket.

"You sneaky, lying witch!" Winston whispered to himself, furious and feeling utterly betrayed. He glanced around the laboratory. "I knew it! I knew she was holding back!" he exclaimed as he eyed the ampoules. He stuck his tiny rat paw into the basket and pulled out a handful of the ampoules. He shoved them in his pouch. Realizing that his paw could only hold about four or five ampoules, but his pouch could certainly hold more, considering it was surprisingly deep. He repeated the process two more times, hiding fourteen to fifteen ampoules. "That ought to do the trick." He grinned. Seeing that he created a small dent in the pile that filled the basket, he rearranged the ampoules as any logical thief would, showing no sign that he had taken any at all. He looked around one last time, before skittering off the table and continuing his search for an escape out of this lair.

Winston searched under the table, running to each corner of the room and stopped in front of an intricately designed brass air vent to catch his breath. He leaned his back up against it, and to his surprise, the wall moved backward, allowing the smallest opening. Winston immediately scurried through the opening and found himself in the laundry room behind the dryer. He peeked around and saw that the coast was clear. He leaned his back against the wall, closing the escape route. He knew he had to find somewhere to hide the ampoules. Sniffing, scurrying, and searching, he finally saw the perfect spot. A small white plastic trash can between the washing machine and dryer. He peered into it and saw a few used dryer sheets and some balls of lint taken out of the dryer's lint trap and thrown away. Winston pulled it all out of the trash can and then emptied his pouch. Once all the ampoules were safe and sound in the bottom of the trash can, he put the dryer sheets and lint back hiding them. Sly rat that he was, indeed. He grinned and then did a couple victory laps around the laundry room, popping a few of the floating bubbles that filled the space. He then easily slipped out under the door. He carefully glanced around the kitchen and saw no one, so he emerged. He was really quite proud of himself and, to tell the truth, downright giddy with the knowledge that he had found Lonora's secret place and took enough poisonous ampoules to get his mother completely out of his way. Chloe would be going to the bazaar with Liam, and with her out of the house, it would be the perfect time to eliminate Julia. Nobody could stop him now.

Honestly, the exorbitantly expensive beach house was not even an issue to him anymore, just the money. He knew that once he had killed Julia, he would manipulate Chloe into giving him all the money that his mother spent a lifetime saving. Chloe would happily hand everything over to him, and he could afford to have whatever he wanted, whenever he wanted. Though he knew he was doing something terrible to get it, he figured that his conscience would be eased every time he looked at his multimillion-dollar bank account. Ah! The power of the almighty dollar.

Chapter Twenty-Six

Chloe sat at Julia's bedside, eyes filled with worry, stroking the little girl's hair as she slept soundly and snoring ever so quietly. Goliath was lying next to her, taking a catnap with his hand resting gently on Julia's shoulder, just as his paw would rest on her shoulder when he was a massive Highland Lynx. Chloe sighed and turned when she heard the door open.

"How is she doing?" Winston whispered, continuing to play the part of the doting son.

"Same, no change at all. She is sleeping," Chloe answered quietly turning her attention back to Julia.

"Something smells delicious. Is it snack time?" Goliath opened his eyes, yawned, and stretched. "Oh, it is just you," he said when he noticed Winston, who rolled his eyes at Goliath.

"I will sit with her, why don't you just take a break." Winston took a step forward, but stopped when Goliath hissed at him as he got off the bed and walked toward Chloe.

"Stop it, Goliath! I have done nothing to deserve such a nasty reaction from you," Winston snapped.

"Winston, you are a rat, I am a cat, it is a habit, it is nature, it is all about the circle of life."

"You are not a cat anymore, Goliath, and this is not wild kingdom, for Pete's sake," Winston responded, knowing that it would sting to remind Goliath that he was no longer what he used to be.

"All right, you two, knock it off. This is not the time nor the place," Chloe whispered.

"Chloe is right, let's take it outside," Goliath told Winston.

"Okay, big man, you want a piece of this, let's go!" Winston trotted out Julia's bedroom door with Goliath behind him; however, instead of Goliath exiting the room, he closed the door and locked it, keeping Winston out of the bedroom.

"He sure is annoying," Goliath said to Chloe, who laughed at his clever maneuver.

Winston stood outside Julia's door with his mouth open after realizing Goliath duped him and locked him out of the room. "Stupid beast!" Winston shouted at the door.

"Who are you yelling at?" Gordo asked, surprising Winston.

"It doesn't matter," Winston told him. "Where have you been?"

"In the garden, isn't it suppertime by now? I am starving. I need real food, Dad, I am sick of vegetables."

"Looks like root hog or die tonight, son…oh, excuse the saying…looks like we will be eating leftovers. Chloe is in there with your grandmother, and I do not think she will be cooking for us tonight."

Winston and Gordo walked into the kitchen, and Winston used every bit of strength he had to open the refrigerator. Once it was open, Gordo stood on his hind legs and stuck his pig snout in it. Using his snout and tusks, he knocked Tupperware containers filled with leftover food out onto the floor. While Winston and Gordo ate the food that had spilled out onto the floor, Fidel slithered down into the kitchen.

"What on earth are you two doing?" he asked.

"Eating supper, come join us," Winston answered.

"No, thanksssss, I am fine."

"What have you been up to?" Winston asked.

"Ssssspending time with Lonora. She is giving you another ampoule ssssoon," Fidel answered.

"Good," he replied, though he knew it was quite unnecessary now. Winston chose to keep the lab a secret. He knew how much Fidel liked Lonora, and he was not ready to discuss with Fidel what he had found just yet. He knew that Fidel was very passionate with regards to things that he liked, and he knew that if he said anything negative about Fidel's new friend, Fidel would simply become defensive, and an argument would ensue. Therefore, Winston decided to continue with the charade. "I hope she gives me the poison tomorrow, since Chloe will be at the bazaar with that doctor fellow. It would be the perfect time to finish Mother off. Chloe won't be here to interfere."

"Do you think one more will do it?" Gordo asked, spitting food out of his full mouth.

"It better, I am getting sick of dragging this out," Winston answered his son.

"Are you sssstarting to have ssssecond thoughts?" Fidel asked.

"Of course not. As a matter of fact, I do not think I have ever been more determined."

Chapter Twenty-Seven

Julia opened her eyes and blinked. She felt Chloe holding her hand, and she looked down to see Chloe's head on her lap, hunched over in a small rocking chair, sleeping soundly. Goliath was asleep on the floor, and Julia smiled. She felt heavy, and a little confused, but above all she felt truly loved. She knew that Chloe and Goliath most likely never left her side. She squeezed Chloe's hand, and Chloe opened her eyes. She looked up at Julia and smiled.

"Good morning!" Chloe exclaimed, which woke Goliath.

"Good morning, dear." Julia sat up in her bed.

"How are you, Julia? Are you okay? Are you feeling more awake?" Goliath quickly got to his feet and stood next to Chloe, resting his hand on Julia's foot.

"I think so. I do not know what is going on. I do not know what is the matter with me. I have no idea why I am so tired." Julia noticed the look of concern spread across Chloe's face. Julia put her hand under Chloe's chin. "Oh, honey! I am so sorry I scared you."

"It is okay, Nanny. I am so happy to see you bright eyed and bushy tailed." Chloe smiled at Julia, but the worry was still showing brightly in her eyes.

"I am, love. In fact, I think I will get up and get some breakfast." Julia pulled the covers back, but Goliath stopped her.

"No, ma'am. You are supposed to stay in bed, right, Chloe? You are supposed to stay in bed and get rest."

"Nonsense. I feel better, and I will continue to feel better if I get up and move around."

"If you feel up to it, you can get up and I will fix you a bowl of cereal," Chloe told her.

"Perfect." Julia got out of the bed, and Chloe, followed by Goliath, went into the kitchen to fix Julia's breakfast. Upon entering the kitchen, Chloe's attention was drawn to empty Tupperware containers on the floor. She looked at Goliath expectantly.

"Do not look at me, I did not do that," Goliath replied defensively. Chloe bent over and picked up one of the containers and inspected it. She looked at Goliath again, and he shrugged.

"Goliath, this bowl looks like it has been licked clean."

"It was not me," Goliath told Chloe.

"Maybe it was Gordo," Chloe responded as she picked up the empty containers and put them in the sink. As Chloe pulled a bowl down from the cabinet, Julia walked in. Goliath pulled a chair out for her as Chloe filled the bowl with cereal and milk. She placed the bowl in front of Julia, who ate a spoonful as Winston walked into the kitchen.

"Mother?" Winston asked, clearly shocked to see her.

"Winston," Julia answered, swallowing her breakfast.

"What are you doing up? How are you feeling? I thought you would still be in bed." Winston was clearly surprised to see her.

"She is feeling better, Winston," Goliath chimed in sitting at the table with Julia.

"She wanted breakfast," Chloe said as she sat next to Goliath.

"But…," Winston started.

"I am feeling better, much better. I appreciate your concern, son," Julia interrupted him as she continued to eat the cereal in her bowl. Winston watched her carefully for a second and then turned his attention to Chloe.

"What time are you leaving?" he asked. He knew that Chloe would be going to the bazaar with Liam, but he needed to know exactly what time she would be out of the house. He knew today was the day he was going to finish this, but he needed Chloe out of his way.

"Leaving? Where are you going?" Julia asked.

"Liam invited me to go to the bazaar with him this evening, but if you are still feeling—"

"Nonsense, dear. I am fine, you go with Liam," Julia interrupted Chloe.

"All right. Liam said he would pick me up at five thirty this evening. I will throw a stew together in the Crock-Pot and you all can have that for supper," she answered Winston's question.

Winston nodded and fought back an evil grin. This was perfect timing, and what was even better was that Chloe had already planned on what to have for supper, so it would be quite simple for Winston to empty the ampoules into Julia's stew. Winston watched Chloe as she put the stew together in the Crock-Pot. Goliath licked his lips as she tossed in and seasoned bits of beef stew meat. He was secretly hoping she would drop a piece or two, or maybe even four or five, on the floor, which he would happily take care of for her. As she put in mixed vegetables, onions, and diced potatoes. Julia finished her cereal and tipped the bowl up to drink the remaining milk.

Chloe added beef stock to the stew, put the lid on the Crock-Pot, and turned it on low. She looked at the clock. "Stew should be ready by five thirty," she announced. The group left the kitchen. Goliath went to visit Amethyst, Julia decided to do a little painting since she was feeling so much better, Chloe went to her room to pick out what she was going to wear to the bazaar that evening, and Winston went to find Fidel and Gordo.

Winston found them both sleeping in the music box room. Gordo had drool oozing out of the corner of his mouth, dripping off his tusk, and he was snoring quite loudly. So loudly, in fact, he was drowning out the soft waltz that was playing. Winston eyed the ballerina, wondering if Lonora was the one truly spinning slowly on the pedestal.

"Winston?" Fidel asked, startling him.

"Oh! I thought you were asleep," Winston said in a whisper so as not to wake up Gordo.

"Who could sleep with that racket?" Fidel asked Winston, referring to Gordo's incessant snoring. Fidel continued, "Further, I do not know why you are whispering. A trash truck could not wake him up."

"How did you sleep?" Winston asked, smiling at Fidel's comment.

"Okay, I suppose. How about you?"

"Never better." Winston was still watching the spinning ballerina.

"She is not here, Winston. She said she was going to go for a swim then watch Chloe and make sure she is still cluelessss. She said she would have the next dose for you in time for ssssupper."

"Excellent! Chloe has created a stew and put it in the Crock-Pot, so she has already taken care of supper. We will have Goliath serve it up."

"Making Goliath an unwitting participant. Winston, you are perfectly wicked," Fidel slithered around happily, and Winston grinned.

As the time drew closer to five thirty, Chloe busied herself getting ready to spend the evening with Liam. She felt nervous and excited at the same time. She was looking forward to spending time with him, but she was also trying desperately, unsuccessfully however, to keep her romantic feelings for him in check. She slipped into a baby-blue broomstick skirt and a matching T-shirt. She grabbed a black cardigan out of the closet and slid her feet into her black sandals.

While Chloe was getting ready, Winston was preparing himself to pour the ampoules he had taken from Lonora's laboratory into Julia's supper. He went to the laundry room and filled his pouch with the ampoules he had hidden in the little trash can. He scampered back into the kitchen and hopped up onto the counter where Chloe had left the bowls for the stew. Winston looked around to make sure nobody was watching him. He reached into his pouch and poured half the ampoules into an empty bowl. He scampered to the Crock-Pot, and with a great deal of difficulty, he lifted the lid. He picked up one of the spoons that Chloe had left out and dipped it into the delectable meal his niece had created. He poured some of the broth into the bowl and gave it a little stir. He had decided that he would tell Goliath that he attempted to get some stew for Julia but was unable to do so given his current physique. Knowing how Goliath felt about Julia, he would happily dish up the stew and serve it to her. Winston then smelled the bowl and twitched his whiskers. It smelled absolutely delicious. Winston went ahead and poured all but two ampoules into the bowl and added a little more broth. His plan would work perfectly.

While Winston was working diligently to poison his mother, Lonora went down into her laboratory. She glided down the steps humming a tune to herself. She stopped at the bottom of the staircase and her eyes scanned the dark room. The cauldron was bubbling, the red sparkles were floating in the air. Though everything seemed normal, Lonora could tell that something was off, but what? She slowly walked to the shelves and studied everything that was on them. Nothing seemed out of place. She walked over to the cauldron; the potion looked perfect. Lonora then walked over to the next set of shelves and that is when she saw it. The opossum tongue. The opossum tongue was not where it belonged. It had been moved. Lonora turned and walked over to the basket containing the extra ampoules. She ran her hand over the basket. A light flickered in her eyes, and they went from charcoal black to an amber flame in an instant. Someone had found her special laboratory. Who was down here? It could not have been the little girl; she was too weak. It could not have been the old woman for she was too concerned about the little girl. The man was following the old woman around like a shadow, just as concerned about the little girl's failing health. The pig was a clueless, clumsy oaf, and the snake was visiting with her off and on all day. Black flames erupted from Lonora's hands and thunder roared, for she was consumed of not only betrayal but of absolute rage.

"You conniving, lying, backstabbing rat!"

Chapter Twenty-Eight

Julia had just finished a painting of a stunning sunset with yucca silhouettes. She was putting everything away and cleaning up when she yawned and stretched out her back. She was suddenly very tired again. She went upstairs from the studio and into her bedroom. She crawled into bed and yawned again. Chloe walked by her bedroom with an armload of dirty laundry and saw Julia lying down in her bed.

"Nanny? Are you doing okay?" Chloe asked, standing in the doorway of Julia's bedroom.

"Just tired again," Julia answered pulling her blankets up around herself as she got comfortable.

"Maybe I should stay home."

"No, absolutely not. Go, have fun, find the vial needed to get us back home. I am just going to rest."

"Yeah, I will take good care of her," Goliath said, coming up behind Chloe and slipping around her as he walked into the bedroom and sat at Julia's bedside.

"You see? I am in excellent hands, Chloe. Goliath will take perfect care of me. When are you leaving?"

"In just a little bit, I thought I would toss in a load of laundry before Liam gets here, he should be here soon."

While Chloe, Julia, and Goliath were talking, Winston was finishing up his perfect plan. He had two ampoules left and decided to make his mother a perfect cup of tea. He poured the poison in the bottom of a teacup and dropped in a tea bag. His ears perked and turned as he heard someone approaching. He put the empty ampoules in his pouch and leapt off the countertop. He ran as fast as he could, on all fours, and slid under the door into the laundry room, doing a perfect swan dive into a pile of dirty towels on the floor next to the washing machine. He was panting and listening intently. He heard footsteps approaching and then heard the door open. He could hear Chloe humming. Winston then heard the sound of the washing machine door opening, and then suddenly, Winston was swept up off the floor along with the pile of towels he was hiding in. Before he could say a word, Chloe inadvertently tossed him and the towels into the washing machine along with the laundry she came in with. She closed the washing machine door and tossed a laundry soap pod into the tiny dispenser and turned the machine on. Chloe heard the sound of a muffled scream. She turned and looked behind her but saw nothing, and then she heard it. The sound of thumping in the washing machine. She turned her attention to the machine just in time to see Winston hurled and smashed up on the glass window on the front of the washing machine door—his tongue protruding, all four paws spread out and pressed against the glass, his one visible eye wide and in horror.

"Oh, my word!" Chloe exclaimed as she hit the pause button on the washing machine. Winston slowly slid down the front of the glass window as the machine stopped running. Chloe quickly opened the door and pulled Winston out.

"Chloe! You idiot!" Winston was gasping, coughing up soap bubbles and gagging on what soap was still in his mouth.

"Uncle Winston, I am so sorry," Chloe said, trying desperately not to laugh as she could not shake the sight of the rat smashed up on the window of the washing machine.

"What were you thinking?"

"Me? What were you doing in the washing machine?"

"I was not in the washing machine, I was in the pile of towels, you moron!"

"Well, what were you doing in the pile of towels then?"

"That is not important, what is important is that you almost killed me," Winston answered as he shook himself out. They both walked out of the laundry room, and Chloe poured boiling water into the prepared teacup. She picked it up and was about to take a sip when Winston shouted at her, "Chloe, stop!"

Chloe jumped and put the teacup back on the counter. "Good grief! What?"

"That tea is not for you, that tea is for my mother!" Winston scurried back up on the counter just as the doorbell rang. Chloe rolled her eyes and walked to the door. Winston let out a sigh of relief and then hiccupped—a bubble popped out of his mouth. He hopped off the counter and ran up behind Chloe as she answered the door.

Liam looked dashing in a pair of khaki slacks and a navy-blue button-down shirt.

"Hi." Chloe smiled.

"Good evening, you look quite stunning," Liam responded, and then looked down noticing Winston. "What happened to you? You look like a drowned rat!" he told Winston.

"I almost was!"

"Just let me say bye to Nanny and Goliath. Come on in." Chloe turned and quickly walked down the hallway into Julia's room. "I am leaving. Supper is in the Crock-Pot, and Winston made you a cup of tea. He is in a foul mood. I accidentally threw him in the washing machine. I think he is okay, but—"

"You what?" Julia asked wide-eyed but with a very big smile on her face.

"It was purely by accident, and I got him out as quickly as I could, so I believe he is okay. Bye, Nanny." Chloe leaned down and kissed Julia on the forehead as Julia laughed at just the thought of the washing machine mishap. Chloe smiled at her, turned on her heel, and left the room. She joined Liam in the living room, and they both left the house.

As soon as Winston heard Liam's vehicle drive away, he scurried to Julia's room, still drenched and hiccupping soap bubbles.

"Winston!" Julia exclaimed as she and Goliath both looked at him. Goliath clapped his hand over his mouth and turned away to hide the hysterical laughter that was about to erupt.

"Do not ask!" Winston replied. "Goliath, can you help me serve Mother her stew, and I made her a cup of tea."

"Sure," Goliath got up and with Winston went into the kitchen.

"I tried to put stew in this bowl for her here but could not get it done in this body."

"No problem," Goliath said. "I can do it."

"Excellent, and I prepared this cup of tea for her."

Goliath dished up the stew and put it on a tray along with the cup of toxic tea. He carried it to Julia, serving her a fatal meal without even knowing it.

Chapter Twenty-Nine

Snickerdoodle was abuzz with the familiar sounds of a joyful community event. The sky was aglow from the lights of the carnival rides that had been set up. Ferris wheels, carousels, even a small roller coaster. Chloe smiled when she heard the laughter of the children and the joyful screams of people on the roller coaster. The air was filled with the smell of cotton candy, funnel cakes, and of course, freshly baked cookies. Vendor booths lined the sidewalks of the little town. There was even a large stage and dance floor set up for live music, and even the snippy pixies seemed to be having a good time.

"Wow! You were not kidding about this bazaar being a big deal. It looks like the entire town is here," Chloe said.

"Yeah, come on, let's go check out the booths," Liam replied taking Chloe's hand in his. Chloe felt the familiar butterflies in her stomach at his touch again, but she did not pull away.

The couple walked down the street and in and out of booths. Chloe eyed the handmade jewelry in one booth. Necklaces and bracelets made from silver and bright rubies and turquoise stones. Another booth showcased delicately etched crystal artifacts such as vases, decanters, and matching drinking glasses. They walked through a woodcarver's booth and smiled at the personalized birdhouses and wall hangings he created. A vendor was selling handwoven rugs and blankets, another had handmade jewelry boxes. The food vendors were pushing their delectable treats like roasted corn, boiled peanuts, homemade candy and cakes.

Liam and Chloe walked into a booth filled with vials. Excitement filled Chloe. This was the most promising booth yet, the most promising locale for that matter. She inspected each one, looking for the vial with the sapphire stone that would send her home and back to her life. Though she always thought her life was quite boring and noneventful, she longed for the blissful normalcy of it.

"Excuse me, sir," Liam addressed a man, who looked ancient with wire-rimmed glasses and a bald head, with the exception of the silver tufts of hair on each side of his head, "we are looking for a very specific vial. It is a tiny sapphire-blue-and-gold vial made of glass." Liam looked around the booth to try to find a similar vial. Chloe walked up to him and handed him an identical vial with an emerald in the center of it rather than a sapphire or ruby. Liam took it and showed it to the man. "Exactly like this one, except for the stone, sir, the one we need has a sapphire instead of an emerald. Do you have what we are looking for?"

"Ah, I am afraid I do not. Unlike a lot of the folks here, I do not make these things, I excavate them. For instance, this pot." The man gently picked up a terra-cotta pot with hieroglyphics on it. "This pot was found at the base of Mount Catherine." He put the pot down and picked up a small ring. "This lovely ring I found buried in the sand about half a mile from the Great Pyramid of Giza. Here, beauty, try it on." The small fellow slipped the topaz ring on Chloe's right ring finger.

"It is beautiful, but…," Chloe started.

"Are you the only vendor here that sells these Egyptian artifacts?" Liam asked.

"Yes, sir, can I interest you in the emerald vial? I will give the ring to your wife for no charge."

"How much is the emerald vial?" Liam asked. He hated to not do anything for the kind man, and the ring did look exquisite on Chloe's delicate hand.

"Twenty dollars, sir."

"Done." Liam handed a twenty-dollar bill to the gentleman, and he and Chloe left the booth with the vial in a small paper bag.

"Thank you for the beautiful ring, Liam, I love it." Chloe smiled at Liam, though she was slightly, only slightly, disappointed that they did not find what they were looking for.

"You are very welcome, Chloe." Liam smiled adoringly at her.

They walked in and out of the remaining booths and were unable to find the Ealim Mthali. Chloe and Liam sat on a stone bench next to a concrete pad at the base of the stage and watched as a band tuned their instruments and prepared to play.

"Do you dance?" Liam asked Chloe as the band began to play familiar classic country songs.

"I do. I love to dance," Chloe answered.

"Then, shall we?" Liam took Chloe's hand and led her to the concrete pad where others had gathered and were two-stepping to the beat of the music. Chloe and Liam smiled at each other, and she followed his lead, guiding her across the dance floor.

"You are an excellent dancer," Chloe said over the loud music.

"As are you, my lady." Liam smiled at her. He was so in love with this woman, this woman who did not belong here, but he did not care. She may not belong in this world, but there was not a doubt in his mind that she belonged with him—she belonged by his side and he by hers.

The band ended their two-step and started playing and singing a slow ballad. Liam held Chloe close as they slowly swayed to the music. Chloe looked up at him, deep in his eyes, and Liam leaned down and kissed her deeply. Chloe pulled away and laid her head on his chest. He held her tightly as they finished dancing to the rest of the song. She was in love with him, and she could not deny that any longer. Perhaps going home was not possible. Perhaps she was exactly where she was supposed to be. The song ended, and Liam and Chloe walked off the dance floor hand in hand. They walked down the sidewalk a bit, and Liam pulled Chloe closer to him. He kissed her again, and she pulled away.

"Liam…"

"Chloe, please. Please do not tell me that this is an impossible relationship. I know that. I know it is, but I would rather have a month, a week, a day, an hour, even one minute loving you than a lifetime without you. I love you, Chloe Graham, I love you."

His words were so sincere. The way he looked into her eyes, her heart melted, and tears touched her eyes as she whispered, "I love you too, Liam." At that moment Chloe did not care if they found the vial. She did not care if they ever went back to the world from which they came. There was no more longing for the life she once had. She had believed she was destined to be single. She was convinced that there was no man up to her standards. The perfect man did not exist, and she was content living with her grandmother in her little house. No, she did not think she would ever find the man of her dreams, and she was right, because the man of her dreams lived in a world she never knew existed.

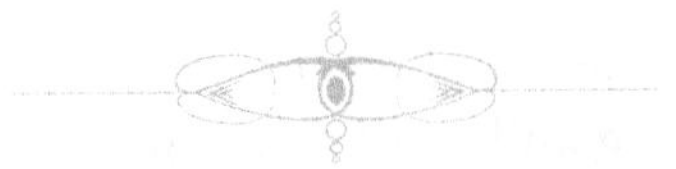

Chapter Thirty

Amethyst stood in the garden, arms lifted up midway at her sides, palms up, and eyes closed with a lavender hue glowing completely through her. Every figurine, every bench, every lattice were floating and flying above the ground and around her. Butterflies, dragonflies, and bluebirds surrounded her. The garden was full of her magical power. She opened her eyes, lowered her arms, and the figurines, benches, and lattices landed gently to the ground and in their rightful place. The lavender glow dissipated, and the butterflies, dragonflies, and birds floated away. Amethyst smiled, knowing that not only were her powers back and in full force, but they were stronger than ever before.

"And so it begins," Amethyst said to herself.

While Amethyst was preparing herself for the inevitable, something horrible was happening inside the house. Julia was in the bathroom with her little head over the toilet. She had been vomiting for several minutes. As she was sick, she was being watched. She was being watched carefully by a mermaid who was enraged as she knew for sure that Winston stole the ampoules from her laboratory. Goliath walked in and hissed at the wallpaper. The mermaid quickly swam across the wall and disappeared behind a shower curtain.

"Julia, are you okay? You sound like you have a hairball. Do you have a hairball?" Goliath asked concerned. He would get sick because of hairballs from time to time, and he firmly believed that hairballs were the bane of his existence. He knew how miserable hairballs made him feel, and he would not wish that on anyone that he loved. He might wish it on Winston or Fidel, but he certainly would not wish it on Julia.

"I must have a stomach bug. I was lying in bed trying to rest, and I started perspiring and feeling very nauseous. I ran in here and have been…" Julia was interrupted by another wave of sickness. "How do I have anything left in my stomach?" Julia asked when she was done. Goliath trotted to the kitchen and grabbed a glass and filled it with water. He brought the glass to Julia. She took it thankfully and rinsed out her mouth. "Okay, I think that might be it." Julia stood up slowly. "I am dizzy." Julia staggered a little bit, and Goliath picked her up.

"I will get you to your bed. You should lie down." Goliath carried Julia to her bed and laid her down. He pulled the blankets up over her. "Do I need to call a vet?"

"No, Goliath, thank you. I think I just need to rest. I am sure I just caught a stomach bug. Probably just a twenty-four-hour flu. I will be fine, just need to rest," Julia said with her eyes closed. Goliath nodded and pulled up the chair next to Julia. He sat down next to her and watched her closely. He had promised Chloe that he would take care of things while she was gone, and he intended to keep that promise.

Winston walked into Julia's room, nose and whiskers twitching as he caught a specific scent in the air.

"Do you smell that? It smells metallic. What is that? Do you smell it?" Winston asked as he quietly walked closer to the bed.

"Yes, I smell it. It is sickness. Julia's not feeling well. She said she thinks she has a twenty-four-hour flu. I think I should call a vet."

"First of all, humans do not see vets, they see physicians. Second of all, if it is just a flu, there is nothing a physician could really do about it. She just needs fluids and rest. Is she running a fever?" Winston asked, acting as concerned as Goliath truly was.

"What is a fever?"

"I will check," Winston replied. He jumped up on Julia's bed and put his muzzle to her head. "Nope. No fever. She probably ate something that made her sick. When she wakes up, you and I can fix her some soup."

"Okay," Goliath said, truly frightened. He believed wholeheartedly that Chloe would never forgive him if something happened to Julia while she was gone.

Winston sat on the bed watching Julia carefully. This was it. This was what he had been waiting for. He could not help but think he could speed the process along with one of the pillows on Julia's bed if he could get rid of the cat, but it was unlikely as he could see the concern on Goliath's face. He then had another idea as his impatience got the best of him.

"Goliath, maybe you should go to the bathroom and wet a washcloth with cool water. We will put it on Mother's head in case a fever does develop. It will be best to keep her cool," Winston said. Though Goliath did not understand the logic, he did as he was told. Winston waited a beat until he was certain Goliath was out of the room. Winston scurried around Julia and grabbed a pillow with his scrawny rat paws. He took the pillow and was about to put it over Julia's face when Goliath walked in with the washcloth.

"What are you doing, Winston?" Goliath asked suspiciously.

"Oh, that was fast!"

"What are you doing?" Goliath asked again as he put the cool rag on Julia's forehead. Julia never moved. Her eyes did not open, and she was slowly but surely fading away.

"I was just fluffing this pillow to put under Mother's head."

Goliath took the pillow from Winston and placed it gently under Julia. He watched her carefully, and he took her hand in his. "You just rest, Nanny. Just rest and you will be okay," Goliath said.

Liam pulled up to the house and opened the pickup door for Chloe. He held her hand as he walked her to the gate. He gently kissed her good night and told her he would call her. She smiled and walked into the house, sighing happily and closing the door behind her when Goliath came rushing out of the bedroom.

"Chloe! Oh, Chloe! I am so glad you are home! Come quick! Something is quite wrong with Nanny, she does not smell good, Chloe!" Goliath was fighting back tears. The joy that Chloe was filled with seconds ago turned to confusion and concern.

"Smell good? What are you talking about, Goliath?" Chloe did not wait for him to answer as she rushed into Julia's bedroom, seeing Julia and noticing that her breathing seemed very shallow. "No! No! No! Nanny?" Chloe dropped to her knees at her grandmother's bedside, and she gave Julia a shake. Her breathing was indeed very shallow, and she was not waking up. "Nanny! Please, Nanny! Wake up! Winston, what happened?" Chloe looked at the rat, panic rising inside of her.

"She seemed fine, she said she thought she had a stomach bug. Goliath said she was sick," Winston said quite nonchalantly.

"Goliath, stay with her. I am calling 911!" Chloe got up and ran to the phone in the kitchen. She dialed the numbers and then heard a familiar tune followed by an absurd message, "The number you have dialed has been disconnected or is no longer in service, please check the number and try again."

"You have got to be kidding!" Chloe exclaimed.

She searched for the number to the doctor, and when she finally found it in the bottom of a drawer, she quickly punched in the numbers. The doctor that had diagnosed Julia with exhaustion answered the phone. Out of breath and panic rising more and more, Chloe explained what she had come home to. The doctor said he would be right over. Chloe hung the phone up and ran back to Julia. Winston was staring at her. Goliath was holding her hand, crying now. He did not know what was wrong, but he could sense that it was not good. Chloe sat on the bed and took Julia's hand.

"The doctor is on his way, Nanny, just hang on. Stay with us, Nanny, please!" Chloe pleaded as tears began to stream uncontrollably down her cheeks.

"It may be too late, Chloe," Winston said quietly.

"What are you talking about? Winston! What have you done?"

"Nothing, Chloe, nothing at all. She looks seven, but she is really an old woman, and perhaps it is her time. I am just saying, it might be that time. It just might be time to let her go, Chloe," Winston answered quietly, speaking softly and calmly.

"No! I will not let her go! I will never let her go!" Chloe was screaming at the devious rat. "I refuse to believe she is dying. Go away, Winston! Get out of this room, get out of my face, I cannot bear to look at you right now!" Chloe was filled with fear, fury, and heartache. What would she do without this woman whom she loved so much? How would she survive losing the woman who took her in when she was just a baby? The woman who raised her. The only mother she had ever known. The woman she loved more than any other human being on the face of the earth. No, she could not die. Chloe could not take it, she just could not.

"I am sorry, Chloe," Winston stated. Was he talking too much? They say that the only reason murderers get caught is because they talk too much. Was Winston in danger of being revealed? Winston remained silent as he sat and waited with Chloe and Goliath.

It seemed as if hours had passed, though it was only fifteen minutes, when the doorbell rang. Goliath quickly got up and answered the door. He came back in the room followed by the doctor.

Chloe jumped up and rushed up to the doctor when he entered the room. "Oh, Doctor! I am so glad you are here! Look at her! What is wrong with her? She is not breathing normally. I cannot get her to wake up! What is wrong with her? Please! Please help her, I cannot…" Chloe's breath had been sucked out of her as she began sobbing hysterically, and Goliath, not knowing what else to do, wrapped Chloe in a tight embrace while the doctor examined the tiny girl who was slipping away by the minute.

"Hmm," the doctor said scratching his head. "I am so sorry, Ms. Graham," he said somberly.

"What? What do you mean? Sorry?" Chloe looked at him in disbelief, tears still streaming down her face.

"I do not know how to tell you this, but for some reason, she is just slipping away. I do not know why. I do not know what caused it. Her lungs are clear, but her little heart is very weak and that is what is causing her labored breathing. I do not know how to tell you this, but this child is dying."

"She can't be!" Chloe could not control the sobs.

"Isn't there an emergency department we can take her to?" Goliath asked.

"Moving her would be extremely risky, and honestly, I cannot promise she would make the trip," the doctor said somberly. "All I can suggest is prayer, and a lot of it. The Good Lord performs miracles constantly, and perhaps God Almighty is not ready to take her home just yet. Perhaps she will pull through, only time will tell."

Chapter Thirty-One

Winston Graham practically skipped upstairs. He was so full of joy. The doctor informed them that taking Julia to a hospital would be risky and futile. The doctor said the only thing to do was to sit and wait and to pray. Perhaps she would pull through, but it was highly unlikely, and nobody knew that better than Winston. He had succeeded with his plan to eliminate his mother entirely from the equation. He knew that soon he would never want for anything because he would have millions of dollars. Chloe was already distraught, and her distress would continue; therefore, she would not hesitate to hand everything over to him. He would make sure of it. After all, he had already killed one thorn in his side, it would not be any harder for him to kill another one.

Winston sauntered into the music box room, humming a cheerful tune, when he saw Fidel and Gordo.

"It is done!" Winston told them.

"What is done?" Gordo asked.

"Your grandmother is dying, son, it won't be long now," Winston answered, placing his paw on the pig's massive shoulder.

"Ssssso, you pulled it off." Fidel slithered. "I had not realized Lonora gave you the final vial."

"Well…"

Winston was interrupted by roaring thunder, and the music box room became very dark as it filled with black smoke.

"I know what you did, you lying, conniving, backstabbing rat!" Lonora emerged enraged, her eyes filled with the amber flame.

"Whatever do you mean?" Winston asked with a grin as he hopped happily away from Gordo and toward the spinning ballerina.

"You know exactly what I mean! You stole from me! You betrayed me!"

"Look who is talking! You were just dragging this whole thing out. You are the one who was being deceitful, Lonora. You had the ampoules all along, and you were just hoarding the poison when you knew that time was of the essence! You knew—"

"Silence!" Lonora interrupted, pulling her hand up and making a fist. "I told you there was a process, I told you that you had to exercise patience! You are incapable of listening, you betrayed me, and you will be punished!" Lonora opened her fist, palm facing Winston, and red smoke emerged. The fire in her eyes grew brighter and brighter as her evil power, fueled solely by rage and revenge, engulfed Winston in the red smoke. He was screaming and writhing in pain. He could not move; he could not escape. An agonizing and burning sensation filled the little rat's body. His arms and legs stiffened, and he could not even twitch his nose. His beady eyes darted downward toward his feet, and he screamed louder as he realized that Lonora was turning him to stone.

"Silence, I said!" Lonora lifted her other hand, and Winston's mouth snapped shut. He could not open it, though he desperately tried. "You made your bed, rodent, now sleep in it!" Winston's body was stone, and it was edging up over his throat and finally to his head, Lonora never ceasing the power. When the smoke cleared, Winston was no longer the devious, murderous, live rat running around. Lonora had turned him into a figurine made of granite and limestone. When Fidel and Gordo had seen what she had done, they were appalled.

Fidel, furious with what the evil fairy did to his husband, leapt off the floor with fangs protruding and ready to dig in, but as he was about to strike Lonora, she put her hand up and he stopped in midair. Fidel's scaled snakeskin began to shed away, beginning at the tip of his tail, piece by piece, and underneath each scale was hard stone. Each scale shed away revealing granite rock. Slowly and painfully, there was nothing Fidel could do. Not even hiss. Each scale fell off the serpent, revealing solid rock. Once the serpent was completely shed of his skin, he was nothing more than a statue, which fell to the ground with a thud.

Gordo squealed as he watched Lonora turn his family to stone. He lunged at her, prepared to use his tusks to rip her apart, but she stopped him in his tracks.

"You have a choice, piggy, piggy. You can be my pet or a decorative ornament to this room." Lonora looked deep into Gordo's eyes, flames growing brighter and brighter, and Gordo's eyes grew wide with terror. Lonora tilted her head and smiled evilly. "Suit yourself." She twisted her hands and surrounded Gordo with red smoke, just as she did with Winston, and he, too, began to change. His tail, his hoofs, his gluttonous body, his ears, his snout, and finally his eyes—granite and limestone.

While Lonora was exacting her vengeance, Goliath was upstairs in his and Chloe's bedroom pacing back and forth, wringing his hands and talking to himself in front of the shelves housing the Fabergé eggs and snow globes. He was so very upset, worried about Chloe and distraught with the news of Julia's current state.

"This is terrible, just terrible! What can I do? How can I help? Why is this happening?" Goliath questioned as he walked to and fro, biting his nails. He spun on his heel, and as he was turning, his elbow hit one of the Fabergé eggs, and all three of them fell to the floor, in a domino effect, shattering. "No!" he exclaimed. "Not again! I am such a clumsy oaf! I cannot do anything right!" Goliath kneeled on one knee and started cleaning up the shards on the floor when something caught his eye. The first thing he saw was the blue sapphire, and his eyes widened when he realized it was a golden vial with the gorgeous stone in the center. Goliath had inadvertently found the Ealim Mthali! It was the vial they had been searching for all along. It was hidden in a Fabergé egg in the bedroom the entire time, right under their noses!

Goliath stood up and slipped the vial in the pocket of his slacks when he heard booming thunder and the sound of glass shattering as if something had been hurled through a window. Goliath felt the house shake. Curious and scared at the same time, he peeked out the bedroom door and down the hall. He saw flashes of lavender light as if a purple lightning storm was erupting in the music box room. The battle between Lonora and Amethyst had begun.

Chapter Thirty-Two

Lonora smiled at the rock garden for which she created in the music box room. She stood upright and cracked her neck. She lifted her palms to vanish from the room and was surprised to see that her hands were trembling. Lonora felt something wet on her upper lip and touched the wet spot with her fingers. When she moved her trembling fingers away from her face, she blinked at the sight of crimson blood that covered them. Her nose was bleeding again. Lonora touched the tip of her nose with her index finger and the blood disappeared. Lonora was disturbed, downright frightened. Why did this keep happening? She felt something deep inside. She felt uneasy, which did not make sense to her since she believed herself to be the most powerful creature ever created. After all, just look at what she had done to her animal friends. She looked toward the window in the music box room just in time to see the window shatter. Shards of glass flew across the room and wind was blowing in so hard that it ripped the velvet drapes down from the wall and flung them to the other side. Lonora's black hair whipped across her face, which was deforming against the wind as if she were sitting in a roller coaster, careening down at an excessive rate of speed. Thunder roared so loud, the house shook, purple lightning flashed, and rising up from the ground outside, as if being lifted by an invisible pedestal, was a beautiful and very powerful fairy. Her pupils were not visible among the lavender glow that filled her eyes, her auburn hair flowed in the strong wind as did the shimmering lilac gown she wore.

"Amethyst! It can't be!" Lonora exclaimed in horror.

"Hello, Lonora," Amethyst responded as she entered the room.

"How—"

"It is time for you to leave, Lonora. You have worn out your welcome, my old friend," Amethyst interrupted her, speaking calmly and softly as she entered the room, landing gently with her feet on the floor.

Lonora cackled, wickedly and loudly. "You fool! How very refreshing though. It is so refreshing to know that some things never change."

"Oh?" Amethyst asked.

"Your gentle spirit is what got you trapped in that tree in the first place. Your naive kindness and absurd benevolence. Amethyst, Amethyst. I do not know how the heck you got out of that tree, but what I am about to do to you, well, darling, you will never be able to come back. Let us end this, once and for all." The flames emerged in Lonora's eyes again as she lifted her hands toward Amethyst to obliterate her. Red and black smoke billowed as a stream of lime green light flew from Lonora's hands, but Lonora was unprepared for Amethyst's defense.

Amethyst raised both her hands and caught the lime green stream, lightning flashed, and thunder roared as she caught the stream and shot it back to Lonora, followed by a magenta stream of power. Sparks flew, and they were followed by glittering lights, looking as if the room was filled with tiny dancing stars. Both streams went straight to Lonora's head, and she back bended as the lights sliced her left cheekbone, causing her to scream in agonizing pain. She was about to stand up when a second flash sliced her right cheekbone. Lonora shrieked again as the burning sensation of a deep cut filled her face. She stood straight and placed both of her hands on her face over the thin wounds and eliminated the gashes. She drew back and threw double strands of powerful green light to Amethyst, who spun around to the left to dodge the blow, you could hear the swooshing of her gown as she turned. Then another double hit from Lonora, and Amethyst spun around to the right, barely missing it. Amethyst threw two magenta balls at Lonora, and she sucked them both up in black smoke. She took a deep breath and hurled the magenta balls back at Amethyst and then followed with a black ball the same size as a cannon ball. Amethyst was not prepared for it nor was she fast enough this time to dodge the powerful orb as it hit her square in the stomach, knocking the wind out of her and thrusting her backward and outside the shattered window where she fell to the ground below.

Lonora released a sigh of relief as she once again triumphed over her nemesis. She slowly walked to the empty space in the wall that used to be a large window through which Amethyst had emerged and fell to her demise. She peered down and was thrown backward, falling to the floor as Amethyst arose again. Her power so forceful that it took Lonora's breath away.

"Things have changed, witch," Amethyst stated when she came to a stop and landed gently on the other side of the room. "I am stronger than you." Amethyst kept her palms out facing Lonora, forcing a lavender hue to surround Lonora to keep her down. "You see, when you trapped me into that tree, I obtained some of your power as well."

Lonora's body was achy and strained. She clenched her fists, straightened out her arms, and with great effort and concentration, broke free from Amethyst's hold. Rising to her feet, she extended her hands. "Only a little!" she exclaimed as she covered Amethyst in black and red smoke.

More sparks began to fly from Amethyst as she fought off the suffocating smoke. She could feel her legs burn and stiffen, causing her to fall to the floor.

"You will be a perfect addition to the stone creatures I have already added to this room!" Lonora laughed as she watched Amethyst's legs turn to concrete.

Amethyst began to panic. Her heart pounded, and she tried desperately to control her breathing. She closed her eyes and focused. Lonora's eyes widened in terror as the concrete began to fade away. Amethyst stood and then floated upward. She swiped her hand toward Lonora, and a purple streak of lightning headed straight for her. She dodged the lightning, diving behind the spinning ballerina on the pedestal. Amethyst threw another lightning bolt toward her, striking the ballerina and demolishing it. Lonora's cackle was wicked and booming as her two arms transformed into legs, like that of an enormous insect. Two more legs grew on each side of her slender body and then one on each shoulder. The legs that grew out of her shoulders ended with large pinchers. Her body became a hard shell and a segmented tail developed with a stinger, sharp as steel, at the end. Lonora had transformed herself into a massive scorpion.

Amethyst was full of fury and glared at the beast, for she was not going to let Lonora win. She would be victorious, even if it killed her.

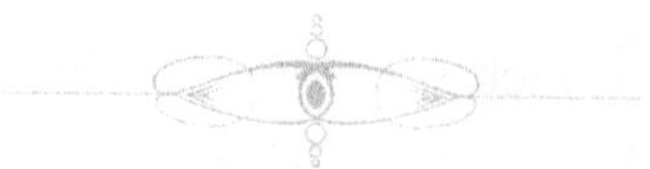

Chapter Thirty-Three

Chloe sat next to Julia, sniffling and wiping away tears, as she watched the little girl's chest move up and down with every shallow breath she took. Chloe was so focused on her grandmother that she jumped when she heard the tremendous racket upstairs and felt the house shake. She looked up at the ceiling and then back down at Julia. She squeezed her hand and kissed her cheek as she stood up and left the room to investigate what was going on upstairs.

"Goliath?" Chloe hollered at the base of the stairs. She waited for a response but just heard thunder clapping and glass shattering. Chloe trotted up the stairs and turned her head to look down the hallway. She saw flashes of purple light coming from the doorway of the music box room. She walked toward it, wondering what in the world was going on. She reached the doorway and caught a glimpse of the giant scorpion in the room. Her eyes widened as the sharp, pointed stinger aimed right at her.

Before she could register what was happening, she heard Goliath holler at her, "Chloe, look out!" Goliath dived and tackled Chloe to the ground, saving her from the deadly scorpion strike.

"Goliath! What is going on? You are going to break my hip!" Chloe shouted. The stinger of the scorpion broke through the wall and struck the floor inches from Chloe's head.

"Run!" Amethyst shouted at Goliath and Chloe.

"Come on, Chloe! Run! We have got to get out of here!" Goliath yelled grabbing Chloe's hand and half dragging her down the hall and to the stairs. Goliath missed a step, and he took Chloe with him as he slid to the bottom of the stairs. He lifted Chloe up by the arms, and they ran into Julia's room closing the door behind them.

"Goliath! What the…"

"It is the battle! The battle that Amethyst told us about! We have got to get out of here! Look, I found the vial to get us home!" Goliath reached in his pocket, but it was empty. Chloe watched him as he turned his pocket inside out, then the other. "Oh, no! I must have dropped it upstairs! No, no, no!" Goliath was panicked as he searched the floor around him. "It has got to be upstairs! Stay here with Nanny, I will go up and find it!" Goliath exclaimed.

"Are you crazy? You cannot go up there!" Chloe grabbed his arm. "You will be killed! It is too dangerous and—" Chloe was interrupted by a small but familiar voice.

"Chloe?" Julia's voice was nothing more than a whisper as she tried to muster the strength to speak.

"Nanny? Oh, Nanny!" Chloe landed hard on her knees next to Julia relieved, but her relief soon faded away as Julia spoke.

"Chloe, promise me," she said.

"Promise what, Nanny?" Chloe gently stroked Julia's hair.

"Promise me you will not consume yourself in grief."

"Grief?"

"I am dying, Chloe. I can feel it." Chloe gasped when the words came out of Julia's mouth. "Do not be afraid, sweetheart, I am not," Julia told her.

"No! No, Nanny, please! Please do not leave me, please stay with me!"

"Promise me you will keep writing. You are a talented writer, honey. Promise me," Julia continued to whisper as she tried to catch her breath.

"Nanny…"

"Promise me you will keep painting," she continued. "You are so artistic, please, promise me." She felt so weak. Julia knew it would not be long now, as it was getting harder and harder to catch her breath. She had to push through enough to tell Chloe what she needed to tell her.

"Nanny…"

"You have been the light of my life, Chloe. You have been my sunshine in the dark, my strength when I have been at my weakest moments, and at times gave me a reason to get up and carry on in the mornings. Promise me, Chloe, that you will continue to shine. You, my love, are destined for greatness." Julia took a deep breath. "I knew it from the moment I laid eyes on you the day you were born." Julia smiled a small smile as Chloe sobbed.

"Nanny, I can't. I can't do this without you! I cannot live my life without you, please do not do this. Please stay with me, Nanny, please!"

"We knew this day would come, Chloe. Nobody lives forever. Oh, Chloe! I love you so much, and I will always be with you. While you are writing, and you hear that little voice that says you are brilliant, know that is me. When you are painting something, and you look back at it and hear how breathtaking the painting is, Chloe, know that it is me. When you go for a walk and feel a pleasant breeze or smile at a song that seems to be stuck in your head. When you feel the warmth of the sun on your face or cannot fight back the urge to dance in the rain, Chloe, that will be me. Kiss me goodbye, Chloe, and let me go."

"Oh, Nanny!" Chloe buried her face on Julia's shoulder and sobbed. "Nanny…Nanny…"

Chloe raised her face as Julia took one last deep breath and then exhaled the last bit of life left in her. Chloe screamed at the top of her lungs as she realized that Julia was gone. Chloe scooped Julia's tiny lifeless body close to hers and held her tightly as if she could simply bring her back to life by sheer willpower. Goliath fell to the floor in grief next to Chloe, who could not hold in the tears, the sobs, the wails that erupted from her. He put his hand on her shoulder and sniffled as he too had tears streaming uncontrollably down his cheeks.

"Chloe…" Goliath did not know what to say. He really wanted to just put his nose up to her, to give her a little nuzzle. Goliath wanted to comfort her, to somehow take away the agonizing pain, to mend her shattered heart, but how could he when his heart was just as broken?

"I can't…Goliath…I can't," Chloe uttered between sobs.

"We have to get home, Chloe…"

"It doesn't matter, Goliath, nothing matters, nothing," Chloe managed. "I do not care. I do not care if we ever leave this place. I cannot live without her! I do not want to live without her!" Chloe wailed, and Goliath embraced her as he cried along with her.

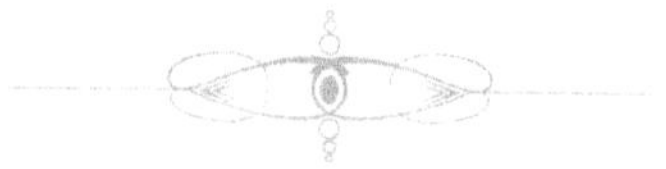

Chapter Thirty-Four

Liam had a sinking feeling as he drove home. He felt anxious. He knew something was wrong, that something was not right. Was he missing Chloe's presence already? He heard a soft voice in his head—it was not Chloe's voice, yet just as sweet. It was almost melodic, yet it was a desperate whisper. Liam slammed on his brakes hard and flipped a U-turn. He thrusted his foot on the gas pedal, pressing it all the way down to the floor of his pickup, speeding back to the only gray house in Snickerdoodle, for Amethyst's concentration on the fight was interrupted by the excruciating pain she felt in her heart. She could feel what was going on downstairs, and it was extremely distracting. Pain! Horrendous pain filled Amethyst's chest as if her heart were breaking into a billion pieces. As she felt Goliath and Chloe's heartache, she knew that she had to summon help. She could not let them suffer alone, and she could not offer them comfort herself, not while she was fighting Lonora. Their pain was so raw, so deep that she had to fight back tears. She closed her eyes, and her mind whispered, "Liam, Chloe needs you now. Hurry, Liam, Chloe needs you."

Liam's brakes screeched as he parked in front of the house. He ran through the gate and up the walk. He did not bother to knock as he grabbed the doorknob and burst through the front door. "Chloe!" he exclaimed. He heard a crashing upstairs. Fearing that she was in peril, he ran up the stairs taking them two at a time.

A fast strike to Amethyst's shoulder brought her back to the matter at hand as Lonora's stinger sliced through her flesh. Amethyst winced at the sharp throbbing pain in her arm as she brought up the pieces of the broken ballerina and hurled them at the scorpion who knocked them away with her long legs. Amethyst lifted Winston and Fidel, now nothing more than heavy stone, and tossed them at Lonora. They knocked holes in the wall as they missed the evil witch. Dust from the debris of the wall filled the room, and when it settled, the scorpion reemerged unscathed. Lonora saw Liam standing in the doorway, jaw dropped and eyes filled with disbelief. She reached out with her long arm and grabbed Liam with her pincher. She squeezed and Liam shouted in pain. The scorpion slung Liam so hard that when she released him, he went through the wall and landed on his back in the hallway, knocking him unconscious.

Amethyst lifted her hands, but before she could release a powerful blow, Lonora whipped her deadly tail at Amethyst's feet and knocked her to the floor. The scorpion rushed toward her, and Amethyst quickly lifted her hand and created a large hedge with giant thorns protruding from it to protect her from Lonora's violent and vicious wrath.

Amethyst lay on the floor for a second, trying to catch her breath and regain her strength. She looked over at Liam lying on the floor, just feet away from her. She could hear Lonora slashing away at the hedge. Amethyst closed her eyes for a beat and sat up. She lifted her hand again creating another hedge and then another, trying desperately to buy herself a little time. She got to her feet and readied herself with her palms facing the protective fence.

"Come on," she whispered, "come on, witch!"

Lonora made it through the hedge, and with a blinding, radiant lilac light, Amethyst put forth as much power as she could at the scorpion. Lonora raised up off the floor and was hurled straight up the room crashing into another velvet-covered wall. Amethyst was not finished with her yet. She slung her to the other side of the room and then bashed her up against the ceiling. Amethyst released her, and Lonora fell to the floor, still and lifeless, transforming back into the sensual vixen.

"My magic is more controlled than yours, Lonora. You said my kindness is my weakness, your hatred is yours. You are too vengeful, too careless," Amethyst said, panting heavily, as she walked slowly to the silent devil woman lying on the floor.

Amethyst limped up to her, weakened and in pain. Lonora did not seem to be breathing, and unbeknownst to Amethyst, she had not fully transformed back to human form. In one quick motion, Lonora turned around and stabbed Amethyst in the stomach with her stinger. Amethyst gasped and her eyes widened as maroon blood poured out of her, like water from a free-flowing faucet. Lonora's laughter boomed throughout the room as she tried to retract her stinger, but then grew silent as Amethyst grabbed it, sucking as much power from Lonora as she could, a barrage of color filled the room. Lavender, black, crimson, and lime green was flashing and glowing around the two fairies. The remaining scorpion tail vanished as Lonora was now fully the evil vixen, and Amethyst collapsed on the floor.

"No, Amethyst, my hatred is my strength. Your kindness was the death of you!" Lonora replied.

"Not yet!" Amethyst exclaimed as she released a final blow of power. Lightning, dark purple fire, and electric sparks flew from Amethyst. The power engulfed Lonora. When the smoke cleared, Lonora was gone. Amethyst lay on her back, screaming and writhing in pain from the poisonous stab wound to her stomach. She placed her hand on her abdomen and could feel the blood pumping and flowing freely. She closed her eyes and black and red smoke billowed from underneath her hand, healing the deadly hole Lonora had caused. She lay there until the wound was sealed. She opened her eyes and breathed.

Slowly, so slowly, Amethyst got up to her feet. She lifted her hands at her sides, and butterflies, bluebirds, dragonflies, and flowers filled the room, completely filled the air all around her. She smiled at the realization that though she took Lonora's power to heal herself, her original power, her beautiful power, was the dominant power.

Amethyst stood for a minute admiring the beauty around her and smiled as a gentle black butterfly with royal blue tips on its wings floated to her and landed on her hand. Amethyst watched it as it fluttered off her hand and was gently flying away.

"You lose, Lonora," Amethyst said as she knew who the butterfly truly was. She pointed at the butterfly and surrounded it in fluorescent pink light. Amethyst guided the butterfly out of the window and into the tree that Lonora had trapped her in so long ago. She took a deep breath and exhaled while the butterfly let out a high-pitched scream being sucked in by the weeping willow. Amethyst closed the witch up in the tree and then smiled at her victory.

Liam moaned as he rolled over and saw the beautiful woman standing before him.

"What the…"

"There is no time, Liam, Chloe needs you now," Amethyst told him.

Liam sat up, and the sapphire-blue stone of a small golden vial caught his attention. He picked it up and looked at Amethyst in awe, for he had found the Ealim Mthali that Goliath had dropped when he rescued Chloe from Lonora's deadly wrath.

"Downstairs, Liam, now," she said.

Chapter Thirty-Five

Chloe and Goliath wept as Chloe cradled Julia's lifeless body in her arms. Amethyst magically appeared on the other side of the room standing next to Julia's bed, tears streamed down her face as she sadly watched Goliath and Chloe deal with the tragedy and trauma before them. Goliath looked up and saw his friend standing at Julia's bedside.

"Oh, Amethyst!" Goliath cried. "It is Nanny…"

"I know, Goliath, I know," Amethyst responded to him in a soft and gentle whisper. Chloe, engrossed in grief, never even glanced up, never even acknowledging anyone else's existence.

Liam raced through the door of Julia's bedroom and was immediately filled with despair as he saw the woman he had fallen so deeply in love with broken and distraught. He looked up at Amethyst who gave him a nod.

"Chloe?" Liam's voice was soft and compassionate. She did not look up at him. Had she even heard him? Did she even know he was there? "I have it. Somehow, I found the Ealim Mthali on the floor in the hallway upstairs…" His words trailed away.

"It is time for Chloe, Julia, and Goliath to go home now," Amethyst replied. "The evil is gone, and this is not their world."

Liam twisted the top of the vial opening it, and he sighed sadly. For a brief second, he considered putting the top back on the vial and destroying it, keeping Chloe here with him forever, but his love for her was so strong, so pure, that he put his own desires aside to do what was best for the woman he believed to be his soulmate.

"I will never find another woman like you, Chloe Graham. I will never love another woman the way I love you. We knew this was how this was going to end. We belong in two different worlds. Goodbye, Chloe." Liam took a deep breath and slowly poured the contents of the vial over Goliath, who was still embracing Chloe, and Chloe, who was still embracing Julia.

Flowing out of the vial was a thick, deep blue liquid. It smothered the three individuals and then evaporated into a foggy dark blue haze. Liam watched sadly, his chin trembling as he fought back tears being produced as a result of utter heartbreak. The sapphire-blue smoke then floated up slowly toward the ceiling, still hovering over Chloe, Goliath, and Julia. It continued to waft into the air until finally disappearing, leaving Liam and Amethyst alone in the room.

"She is gone," Liam whispered, "she is gone, and I guess I have to figure out how to continue on without her. I guess I have to figure out how to live this life without that beautiful creature by my side. I found true love, you know? I finally found what I had been searching for all my life, and now it is gone." Tears began to stream down his cheeks. He dropped the vial, and it bounced off the toe of his shoe, hit the floor, and then shattered into a million pieces, just as his heart was shattered into a million pieces.

"Liam…," Amethyst began.

"It is fine, Chloe warned me this was how it was going to end. I just did not really think about this emptiness I am so very consumed in."

Liam turned to leave; however, upon taking the first step, he vanished as if he was never there in the first place.

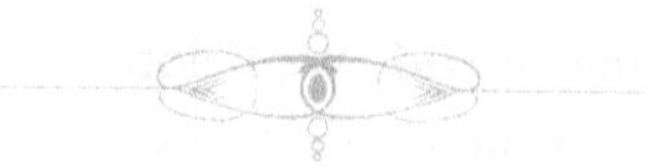

Chapter Thirty-Six

"Meow!" Goliath called out as he nudged Chloe's arm. Chloe felt the familiar sensation of fur on her elbow. She sniffled as she looked down to see her sensational Highland Lynx rubbing up against her arm. She was wearing her satin pajamas and sitting on the floor of the familiar bedroom that her grandmother used to sleep in. Her eyes moved over to her arm, and she saw her hand, no longer aged, no longer wrinkled, but smooth and as it was at what seemed like so long ago. She looked at Julia, still cradled in her arms, wearing a cotton nightgown and no longer a lifeless child, but an eighty-four-year-old woman who had lived a long life, filled with joy and heartache. Stories and memories that would never be forgotten.

As Chloe blinked, she realized she was home. Tears continued to fall, dropping onto her grandmother until…Julia gasped for air, taking in a deep breath, and she slowly opened her eyes.

"Nanny!" Chloe exclaimed.

"Oh, Chloe! I just had the most bizarre dream!" Julia replied.

"Nanny, you are alive! You are alive! You are alive!" Chloe was ecstatic as she clung to her grandmother so tightly.

"Well, I won't be for long if you do not loosen up a little!" the woman announced. Chloe chuckled and released the hold she had on Julia. "I had the strangest dream. I had this dream that everything was topsy-turvy. You were old, I was young, Goliath was a man! In this dream, Winston was a rat, Fidel a snake, and even Gordo was there. He had been transformed into a pig, a big fat pig, Chloe!"

"Nanny, it was not a dream. It was real, it was all real! Goliath found the vial to bring us back home, you were very sick, and you even died." Chloe was speaking so fast that Julia was having to concentrate to understand the words coming out of her mouth. "Goliath found the vial but then he lost it. Liam showed up, I do not really even know when or how, but he found it and he sent us home." Chloe sighed. "You are alive!" Chloe threw her arms around Julia again, truly ecstatic.

"Yes, honey, I am alive," Julia said. "Where is Winston and Fidel? Where is Gordo?" she asked.

"I honestly do not know." Chloe stood up and helped her grandmother to her feet. "They were not in the room with us. It was just you, Goliath, and myself. I guess they are still in Snickerdoodle."

"Snickerdoodle! After everything that has happened, I still think it is a charming name for a town," Julia responded, smoothing out her cotton pajamas. She looked down at Goliath who was rubbing his entire body up against Julia's leg. "And look at you! The most handsome cat I have ever laid eyes on." Julia smiled as Goliath let out a barrage of purrs. "I could use a drink," Julia told Chloe as they exited her bedroom and walked, hand in hand, into the kitchen.

Chloe opened her refrigerator and pulled out the opened bottle of pinot grigio. She poured a glass for herself and one for her grandmother.

"You are old enough to drink this now." Chloe smiled as she handed Julia her glass, and they sat at the table together.

"Well, I think I have certainly earned it, don't you?" she asked as she smiled at Chloe but then stopped as Chloe sighed sadly. Tears touched her eyes.

"What is it, dear?" Julia asked.

"Liam," Chloe answered. "You warned me, I know you did, but I fell in love with him anyway, and now I am heartbroken. I am thrilled to be home, I am overjoyed that you are okay, but my heart still aches for a man I never knew existed, for a love that I never thought I would find." Tears streamed freely as the words left her lips, and she quickly wiped them away.

"I understand, I truly do," Julia said as she rested her hand on Chloe's.

"Life goes on, right? I guess our life just needs to move on. It will be a better life with the rat, snake, and pig out of it." Chloe wiped more tears away and took a drink of her wine.

"Do you think anyone will miss them?" Julia asked sipping her wine.

"Perhaps. If they do, we can say they moved away. They decided to retire. We could say they bought a house somewhere and moved away, perhaps to another country."

"Sounds like a good idea to me." Julia smiled sweetly at her granddaughter, who was still wiping away tears that only came from a love lost.

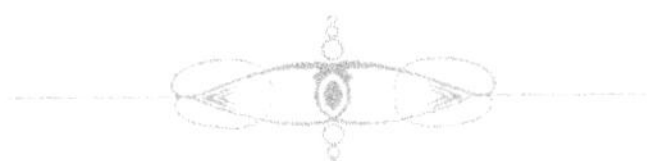

Chapter Thirty-Seven

A month later, Julia smiled as she read the drafted chapter of Chloe's newest book that she was writing. It would be Chloe's debut fantasy novel, inspired by an incident that happened a while back. Chloe entitled it *The Mystic Vial*, and Julia thought it was brilliant. Though the incident was quite factual, nobody would ever believe a world like Snickerdoodle existed, nor would anybody believe that a young woman would be transformed to an old woman. Nobody would ever believe that a cat would be transformed into a human or that an old woman would be transformed into a child. Who on earth would believe that men could change into rats, snakes, or pigs? People believed fairies and pixies to be mythical creatures, and therefore, Chloe was writing her book as fiction.

As Julia read through the pages, Goliath napped on her lap, purring loudly and every now and then would knead Julia's leg. Engrossed in the pages of Chloe's newest creation, a knock at the door caused her to jump, resulting in Goliath to awaken and leap off Julia's lap. She stood up and walked out of the kitchen and to the front door. When she opened it, she was quite surprised to see a very handsome man, with sandy-blond hair and hazel eyes. He looked to be slightly older than her granddaughter.

"Hello," Julia said to him. "May I help you?" she asked, as Chloe, hearing from her home office that someone was at the door, emerged behind her.

"Yes, ma'am," the man answered.

There was something so familiar about him. Chloe stared for a minute. She knew those eyes; she recognized those eyes.

"Liam? It can't be!" Chloe exclaimed.

Julia stepped aside as a much younger Liam Donnelson walked into the house.

"I found you!" Liam responded as he embraced Chloe, who was smiling from ear to ear.

"How did you—"

"The vial, I guess when I dropped the vial and it hit my foot, there was still some potion in it, and I ended up here. Quite younger, and quite confused."

"I know the feeling!" Chloe smiled, and her heart was soaring.

Julia could not help but share in her granddaughter's glee, and Goliath rubbed up against Liam's leg.

"It took me forever, but I found you, Chloe Graham, I found you! I wandered into a restaurant, Coleman's I think was the name of it, and saw paintings painted by a Julia Graham. I asked about them, and it seems that Ms. Graham is a regular at the restaurant and quite popular. The manager at the restaurant told me how to find you when I told him I was in love with her granddaughter. I pleaded with him, as he was quite hesitant, but I made a very strong case, and now here I am, and here you are, and I found you!"

"You found me, and Nanny is alive, and Goliath is back to being the most handsome animal on earth, and I could not be happier right now! All is right with the world right now!"

Liam could not agree more as he scooped Chloe up in his arms and kissed her, deeply and passionately, which she joyously returned the love and affection. Yes, all was right with the world indeed.

It would remain that way until another sweet and innocent soul would be summoned to the magical town of Snickerdoodle. Though the evil was gone, it would not be gone forever. The battle between good and evil had been won, but the war between good and evil had just begun.

About the Author

Stephanie Dean is currently working on the prequel and the sequel to *The Mystic Vial*, making *The Mystic Vial* the second book of a trilogy.

She has been writing for years and is the author of the children's books *Abby and the Fabulous Clubhouse* and *Buster's Braces*, which are the first two books of her "Greenville Animal Friends" series, set in Greenville, Alabama.

Stephanie is also the author of *A Fatal Proposal* and *Sinister Revelations*, the first two books in her "Sam and Hailey" murder mystery series for adults.

She also wrote the inspirational novel, *Victorious Burgandy*, which was released in November 2019, and entered in the Writer's Digest Self-Published Book Awards, for which the judge noted, "The story is incredibly moving. The narrator / main character shares her painful journey with a tone of hope and strength that will, no doubt, inspire anyone who reads the book."

Stephanie has appeared on local news broadcasts as well as being featured on the front page of the *Greenville Advocate*, a local newspaper out of Greenville, Alabama.

Printed in the USA
CPSIA information can be obtained
at www.ICGtesting.com
LVHW041154190924
791248LV00001B/24